Bow Grip

Ivan E. Coyote

ARSENAL PULP PRESS

VANCOUVER

BOW GRIP
Copyright © 2006 by Ivan E. Coyote

Third printing: 2008

ARSENAL PULP PRESS
Suite 200, 341 Water Street
Vancouver, BC
Canada V6B 1B8
arsenalpulp.com

The publisher gratefully acknowledges the support of the Canada Council for the Arts and the British Columbia Arts Council for its publishing program, and the Government of Canada (through the Book Publishing Industry Development Program) and the Government of British Columbia (through the Book Publishing Tax Credit Program) for its publishing activities.

This is a work of fiction. Any resemblance of characters to persons either living or deceased is purely coincidental.

Text and cover design by Shyla Seller
Cover photography by Cheyenne Clegg
Photograph of Ivan E. Coyote by Chloë Brushwood Rose

Printed and bound in Canada

Library and Archives Canada Cataloguing in Publication:

Coyote, Ivan E. (Ivan Elizabeth), 1969-
    Bow grip / Ivan E. Coyote.

ISBN 1-55152-213-6

    I. Title.

PS8555.O99B69 2006   C813'.6   C2006-904646-8

ISBN13: 978-155152-213-5

This book is dedicated to the men in my family.
Especially you, Dad.

I would never have sold him the car in the first place if I'd known what he was going to do with it.

I'd seen him around town a couple of times, once or twice at the café, just drinking coffee, no cream, no sugar, never eating anything, and now and then at Ida's little grocery store, buying crackers and tins of oysters and canned soup, you know, bachelor stuff. I should know.

Once or twice I'd seen him thumbing a ride on the highway, always when I was going the other way, not that I'd have picked him up necessarily, since I've usually got the big dog in the front seat with me, shedding and generally leaving no room for another passenger, something Allyson always used to complain about, before she left. I guess I pretty much inherited my dad's disdain for hitchhikers, and on top of that, I had heard nothing but no good about the guy, if you can believe what you hear around town. My buddy Rick Davis nicknamed him the cowboy, kind of sarcastic-like on account of the straw hat he wears everywhere, combined with his apparent lack of a horse to go with it. Anyways, the cowboy isn't much liked by the guys I play hockey or poker with, nobody trusts him. Rick says it's because the guy doesn't appear to have regular employment and he lives alone in a school bus. I always secretly thought he was unpopular because he's quite good-looking, or so the ladies tell me, and a bunch of paunchy poker players with receding hairlines probably never take too well to an unattached man showing up in town. Nobody invited Nick the new dentist over for dinner for years, until he imported that blonde nurse from Edmonton and properly married her and moved her piano in. Now he's one of the guys, like he's been here in Drumheller forever, just like the rest of us.

I realized when the cowboy came into the shop last month and inquired about the Volvo that I'd never heard him talk out loud at all before that. Not very friendly of me, when you think about it. He's been living out at Archie's farm for going on three years by now, easy, and I guess I've never even said a proper good day to the man.

"Name is Carson. James or Jim. People call me both. Saw the car for sale out front."

His long-fingered paw appeared in the sideways rectangle of light between the concrete and the underbelly of Betty Makerewich's Taurus wagon. I was on my back underneath it, on the dolly, since Franco was using the hoist. I rolled out to shake James or Jim Carson's hand.

"Saw the car out front," he repeated. I didn't so much mind someone getting straight to the point like that. No small talk with this guy, that was plain to see. Some folks just don't like messing around with the idle chatter. There's been days I wished Franco was more like that. I got right to it. I wiped my greasy hand on the thigh of my coveralls and shook hands with him for the first time. His grip was firm, but not one of those look-how-tough-I-am handshakes, the ones that feel like foreplay to a fist fight. Just a decent hello.

"The Volvo," I told him. "Came in on a trade for some work I did. Used to belong to Donny Nolan's oldest daughter. He bought it brand new for her eleven years ago. Single owner, lady-driven. Couple hundred and twenty thousand clicks on it though, from when she was going to film school

8

in Winnipeg, but someone took care of it, for sure, it's still in fine shape. Solid. I'm thinking I want thirty-eight hundred. I rebuilt the carburetor and replaced the head gasket. New battery. Good little car. Lots of rubber left on the tires, too."

We walked out the open bay doors to the asphalt yard in front of the shop, towards the blue Volvo. He didn't stop to kick the tires or open the hood; instead, he opened the driver's side door and folded his long frame inside the leather interior. He ran his palms over the steering wheel, wiggled the gearshift. He had a good four or five inches on me, and he slid the seat back to make room for his legs, and surveyed either himself or the empty back seat in the rear-view, hard to tell from where I was standing.

"You want to take it for a spin?"

He appeared not to hear my question. "Thirty-eight hundred you want? Would you consider a trade?"

I shook my head. "Like I said, I already took it on a trade in the first place. Got to keep the cash flow going somehow."

I had done a lot of work for trades over the years. In a town mostly populated by farmers, ranchers, and hunters, I was often offered things other than money in exchange for fixing up something or other for someone. Too bad I couldn't buy new parts or pay the electric bill with frozen deer meat or cords of firewood. Franco only worked for cash, too.

"Don't have the cash," the cowboy said, his hands still on the steering wheel, ten o'clock and two o'clock, as my dad had once taught me, years and years ago.

"You could talk to the bank then, see about a small loan?" I raised the end of my sentence in a half-hearted question. I knew the guy didn't have a real job. He had built a more than decent deck and fence for Mrs Baker when she got her insurance money, and he helped out at Archie's farm, where he kept his school bus parked, but I didn't think the bank would like him much for a loan.

"Don't have the time. I need the car right now. I need the car tomorrow."

"Well, what do you have to trade for it?" I was hoping it was something I already had or didn't need, so I could say no to him with no hard feelings. Business is business.

"A handmade cello."

"Beg your pardon?"

"A cello. The instrument. You play it with a bow, like a violin, but it's a lot bigger. It's a beautiful piece of work, worth a helluva lot more than thirty-eight hundred dollars. More like five or six. Thousand."

"I don't play an instrument. Never had the knack. Tried playing trumpet in high school. Never took to it."

"Strings are different than brass." He pulled a half-flattened pack of Player's from his jean jacket and pushed the Volvo's cigarette lighter in with a wide thumb. "Much more emotive. You should think about it. A new hobby. Something to fill the time, since your wife left. This car needs a new cigarette lighter."

I took one step back. I thought about being pissed off that this guy who I hardly knew was bringing my private life up into a conversation regarding a used car, but then I remembered what my mom had said to me not the very night before. I had come home from walking Buck Buck to find her sitting on my back porch, a Saran Wrap-covered meatloaf steaming up on the stairs beside her rump.

"There you are," she had said, hauling herself to her feet. "Take this. Your sister and I have been talking about you recently. We worry. We think you need a hobby. You need to move on. You need to clean up Ally's office, and pack up the last of her stuff and send it on to Calgary. She's not coming back, Joseph. Time you faced facts. Got on with things. Get yourself a diary, or build something in your shop, whatever. I'm off to bingo. You need a haircut."

I decided on the spot to trade the guy for the cello. The car had had a For Sale sign in its windshield for six weeks now, with no one showing more than a passing interest in even test-driving it. I could buy myself a new hobby, I figured, and get my mom and Sarah off my case for a bit. All it would cost me was the work and parts I'd already put in to Nolan's tractor, and the labour I had put into the Volvo. I still didn't like the guy bringing my wife's whereabouts up in casual conversation, but I didn't have to like him to do business. The car could sit there for months; I was a mechanic, not a salesman. Instruments were expensive, I knew, because Rick Davis was always bitching about still making the payments on his oldest son's baritone saxophone, and the kid graduated already last June. Five thousand bucks was a lot of cello.

I shook the cowboy's hand for the second and last time. "Bring the thing around tomorrow, I've got the transfer papers for the car in my desk. I'll be here anytime past seven-thirty. You want to take it for a spin then?"

He shook his head, and lit a squished smoke with a silver flip of his Zippo. "I'll take your word that it runs just fine."

Normally I would have mentioned there was no smoking in the vehicle, but I figured, what the fuck? The car was his now, after all, he could smoke in it all he wanted. I never smoke in my own truck, but only on account of the dog.

James or Jim Carson refused my offer of a cup of coffee, saying he had business to attend to and he'd be back in the morning, first thing. I dug out a set of transfer papers, unplugged the open sign, and locked up.

The sun was still working its way over the horizon as I walked the three blocks from my place to the shop the next morning. The lights were on in the office already, and the open sign had been plugged in. The Volvo was gone.

Franco was in his chair drinking coffee on the other side of my desk. The cello was in a black case in the corner, taking up too much room, polished and out of place next to the dusty coffee maker and the wall of calendars, ancient and new. The seller's copies of the transfer papers were in a neat pile in the centre of my desk. Buck Buck circled the rest of the floor, uncertain where he was going to lie down now that the space beside the heater was occupied.

I picked up the cello and stashed it in the closet with the broom and the spare printer paper.

"The guy that lives in that old bus at Archie's place was here half an hour ago," Franco said, flipping the page of his newspaper. "I tried to call you but you must have been walking the beast." He eyed me sideways from his duct-taped rolling chair. "Couldn't see you needing a cello, no offense, but the guy was fairly adamant that you two had made a deal. Seemed too weird not to be true, if you know what I mean. He filled out the papers, and I forged your bit for you, so he could take the car. Said he was in a hurry."

"Thanks, Franco." I poured myself a cup of coffee and added one cube of sugar, stirred it with the pen from my shirt pocket.

"Since when do you need a cello more than you need a perfectly good car?"

I took a slow breath. Like I said, Franco talks too much sometimes.

"Thought I'd get myself a new hobby."

"You don't even whistle."

"A guy can't try something new every once in a while?"

"You listen to all-news radio. I never heard you play so much as the stereo. I never took you for the musical type, is all."

"I don't know if I am the musical type, but my mom is on my case to get a hobby, and the man needed a car, so I took the goddamned cello. Now everyone can be happy. Maybe I'll be good. Maybe I'll be Alberta's next Ashley Mac-Issac."

"He's from the Maritimes. And he plays fiddle. Not to mention he's a flamer." Franco's eyes dropped and I watched the red creep up into his stubbled face. "I'm sorry, Joey."

"Don't apologize to me, Franco." I knew what he was thinking. He was thinking about Allyson, living with another woman in Calgary. He was thinking he had sideways insulted my wife, the lesbian, by calling Ashley MacIssac a flamer. I was getting sick of everybody bringing up my private life as though it were the hockey scores or current events. Even a guy with no phone living on a bus on a farm twenty minutes outside of town had heard all about where my wife had gone and with whom. That could be partly due to who she had left town with. Kathleen Sawyer. Mitch Sawyer owns the Esso on Fourth Avenue, and his wife had been a fairly quiet kindergarten teacher, not much to gossip about at all, until her and Allyson both broke the news to Mitch and me on the same night.

That was a little over a year ago now, and ever since then Mitch has spent at least three nights a week in the lounge of the Capitol Hotel, telling anyone who will sit for a beer with him all about his wife and my wife and their one-bedroom artist's loft in Calgary.

Mitch Sawyer seems to feel that the fact Kathleen left him for another woman is more binge- and sympathy-worthy than if she'd just run off with his brother or the postman, but I guess I don't really see it that way. My wife of five years has left me, and I pretty much don't care who she went with, all I know is that she's gone, and it's been about twelve and a half months now of looking like she isn't coming back. Drinking doesn't seem to help much either, so mostly I try and just avoid running into Mitch Sawyer. I like the Mohawk gas better, anyways, higher octane, plus they got the video rental counter right there in the gas station. I've been watching a lot of movies lately.

I changed the subject by grabbing the clipboard with the work orders off the nail beside the door. "You want to pull a rad on the F-150, or you want to do the transmission in the Subaru?"

"You pissed off at me, Joey? I think it's great you got a cello to learn to play. Take your mind off things."

"My mind is my business, Franco."

"I only say it because you're like family. I told your father I would look after you."

"You told him no such thing. My father thought everyone should look after himself."

"Your father thought a lot of things. You forget, I knew him before there was you. He was like a brother to me. He wasn't like you. Your father, you could carry on a conversation with. He always said you had the insides of your head sewn up like a baseball. Could never figure what you were thinking about."

"Transmission or radiator, Franco?"

"You should loosen up, Joey. You'll end up with that prostrate cancer, like what happened with Archie's little brother. The stress."

"Transmission it is, then." It was eight o'clock. I turned the volume on the news way up, popped the hood on the Ford, and didn't speak to Franco again until we stopped working four hours later. We took our coveralls off and headed over to the café for a bite. Neither of us had gotten around to packing a lunch.

All through my beef dip, the only thing Franco talked about was fishing. No comments regarding wives, his or mine. Franco's wife Claudia had left him thirty years ago, because of the drinking. I remember the whole thing, it happened the summer I turned ten. It was 1974, Richard Nixon was resigning as the President of the United States, they showed us a traumatic video about nuclear war in the gymnasium on the second last day of school, and Franco's wife took the kids and moved into her sister's basement suite. Franco stayed on the pull-out couch in the sewing room at our place for three months. It was just before he came to work for my father. But Franco has never talked about Claudia with me, even when Allyson first left, and I'm not the type to bring things up. Franco talks about women a lot, but never Claudia.

Franco didn't mention Allyson, my new hobby, or my stress levels either. All through lunch he just went on about fishing. Just the same old stories about the ones that got away.

That night I dragged the cello home and laid it down on the loveseat next to the front window in the living room, where Ally used to lay and read on rainy days. I opened the case. Inside, it smelled like an attic, or an old suitcase. The wood was deep red-brown and glowing. James or Jim had shined her up nice for me. There was also a soft rag, a bow with a sweat-worn handle, and a small tin of wax. I didn't take the cello out, just sat for a bit and stared at it. I'd have to get an instruction book out of the library. I reached over and plucked the thickest string. The body of the cello hummed a cement foundation of a note until I placed my hand on it. It felt warm, like a living thing. Like it could breathe on its own, if I could figure how to get it started.

I closed the case and walked into Allyson's office. Her desk was still there, a third-hand solid oak number I had found for her on our first anniversary. There was still a coffee cup sitting on the desk's faded top, the remains of its contents now dried like varnish on its bottom and sides. The cup was orange, Allyson's favourite colour. It had lime green and lemon-coloured flowers on it, like from the seventies. I think it used to belong to my parents. I think we once had the whole set. Ally had probably scooped it from Mom and Sarah's pile of yard sale stuff, when my mom bought the new set from the IKEA in Calgary. Ally loved old stuff. The first real fight we ever had was over the kitchen appliances, when we first bought this place. She loved the Harvest Gold fridge and stove set. My mom thought they were hideous and had to go. I didn't really care either way, they still both worked fine, but I let my mom talk me into thinking we needed a new stainless steel set, and that Ally would love it. I thought Ally would be pleasantly surprised, but instead she wouldn't even let me unload them out of the back of my truck. It hadn't even occurred to me that she would prefer Harvest Gold to stainless steel.

I ended up sitting through a serious lecture about how

it was unhealthy for a grown man to let his mother make decisions for him, and how I was married now and that meant it was my wife's job to tell me what colour the stove was going to be, not to mention that buying new stuff when the old things weren't broken was exactly what would eventually turn the planet into one big toxic landfill, and so on. We ended up cutting a deal. I took the new fridge and stove back the next day, but we got Rick Davis to come put a new hardwood floor in the front room, in place of the orange and brown shag that Ally claimed to love. The guy at the Sears laughed at me when I showed up again the very next morning to return the new fridge and stove, explaining that my wife was attached to the old stuff. He asked me if my wife was from the city, because the vintage look was all the rage these days in Toronto, even Calgary now. Then he tried to sell me a brand new fridge and stove that was built to look old already, from a catalogue. Ally really laughed when I told her that bit later. Said it was painfully ironic, didn't I think? What Ally doesn't know is that the old Harvest Gold stove finally kicked the bucket not a week after she split, and now I have a brand spanking new stainless steel range, right next to the old gold fridge. I still owe Rick Davis free oil changes for a year yet, in trade for part of the labour from him putting in the new floor five years ago, and he's still bitching about paying good money for a baritone saxophone collecting dust in the basement because his fucking kid decided to study political science in college instead. Meanwhile, I'm the only divorced guy around these parts who doesn't have a built-in ice cube maker. Painfully ironic, you bet.

I took the dried-out coffee cup and put it to soak in the sink, cracked a cold one, and went in to the garage. I dug out two plastic bins, emptied out the camping gear inside them onto a shelf, and took the bins into Ally's office. I started packing up her remaining books: mostly school stuff, paleontology, some Jung, and a few novels. Books on gardening, pottery, and beekeeping. She had wanted to keep bees one day, when we sold this place and bought something bigger, farther out of town, somewhere on a lake. We both had a thing about swimming in lakes. Ally had already taken all the cookbooks from the cupboard in the kitchen. She once told me when we first got together, before we even moved in, that she never went anywhere without her cookbooks. She had kept her word about that bit.

The books filled one bin to the top, and three-quarters of another. I took a breath and opened the top right drawer of her desk. I had never even sat down at Ally's desk since I gave it to her, just like she would never have touched anything on my workbench in the garage, or opened mail with only my name on it. It was one of the things about Ally and me that I had always appreciated, that we still had private spaces and lives. No rules or hassles about it, we just fell into things that way. We were both just naturally private people. Not like some couples get. Until she popped the news to me about her and Kathleen Sawyer, of course. That was the first time that her privacy turned itself into a secret, right before my ears.

But my mom was right, Ally wasn't coming home, and besides, she might need some of this stuff in Calgary. She had been pretty busy with school, kept saying she was going to come back for the rest of her belongings, but never seemed to be able to get away from the city. I hadn't been able to bear the thought of this room being empty, and the house feeling definitely too big for one guy, plus I always felt like sending her stuff might seem to her like I didn't want her back, if something didn't work out for her and Kathleen and she ever wanted to come home.

Mitch Sawyer had sold Kathleen's canoe and given her mountain bike away out of spite, to another teacher that Kathleen hated. He told me all this, not two weeks after they had left, like I would be proud of him. Like I said, I mostly try to avoid the guy, except for hockey, where I can't help it. Can't start kicking guys out of the league for being underhanded with their ex-wives, or there might not be enough bodies for a decent game.

The top right drawer contained only pens and pencils and what looked like the charger for her laptop. The bottom drawer was full of files, school stuff like old essays and quizzes, all stacked in no apparent order, just like most of Ally's papers always were. At the very bottom of the drawer was a framed certificate. I wasn't snooping, really, but when I was putting it in the bin I couldn't help but notice that it was a Master's degree, dated 2002, more than a year before Ally had left. Three years into our marriage. In her maiden name, not the hyphenated version Franco had always hassled me about. It was from the University of Alberta, in Edmonton.

I sat back on my heels and thought about the half-pack of stale Player's Lights I kept in the junk drawer in the kitchen. I had been trying to quit, with limited success. But for some reason my wife had apparently spent at least a couple of years of our marriage going back to school and getting her Master's degree in dinosaur bones without ever mentioning it to me, and I suddenly needed a smoke something terrible.

I packed up the rest of her stuff without really looking

at anything, chain-smoking all the while. I dragged the bins out to the garage and heaved them onto the shelf next to the loose camping gear. Then I tripped over the snow shovel, cracked my shin, and cursed all the way back to the fridge for another beer. I parked my ass on the chair in the front room, and turned on the television.

It was just after nine o'clock. I flipped through a rerun of *Law and Order*, past channel after channel of the American election debate, and finally landed on a movie. It was about this woman who was dating two guys at the same time, the one guy was a nice, respectable blue-collar type that her mother wanted her to marry because he was from a good family in the neighbourhood, and the other was a red-wine-drinking writer, a rascal that nobody but the lady approved of. She stands up the nice guy, choosing instead to try and hook up with the drunken writer, because he is of course the guy she is hot for. And the nice guy, he's moping around at home hoping she'll eventually show up. She does, but only after the writer guy acts like a total prick and breaks her heart, and only so her mom won't freak out on her about what was she supposed to tell the nice guy's mother, who was a friend of the family and went to the same temple and all.

I was just about to grab the remote and change the channel, as the plot seemed unlikely to move towards a car chase or even any gunplay or explosions, which is mostly what I was in the mood for, when the nice guy asks the woman if she would dance with him in his kitchen, with the flowers on the table and the volume on the radio turned way up.

I remembered that Allyson used to tell the story of how she knew she loved me by the way she felt the first time she saw me dancing in a kitchen. She figured she could settle down with a kitchen dancer.

I put down the remote.

It happened at my little sister Sarah's thirtieth birthday party, in her and her husband Jean-Paul's kitchen. It was the year before Dad died, Ally and I had been dating for about six months, and this was her first full-on family experience. Jean-Paul had bought Sarah this fancy new CD player unit with detachable speakers, the tabletop kind of model. But it cranked up pretty good and Sarah put on Cat Stevens' "Peace Train." My niece Chelsea was about eight, I guess, and she grabbed my hands and stood on my feet for me to dance around the kitchen with her. Then I danced with Sarah and Chelsea both for a bit, until Chelsea's two little buddies jumped on me, and I had to stop because I nearly threw my back out again.

So the nice guy and the woman are dancing in the kitchen together, and she's having a fairly good time in spite of herself. But she keeps smelling vanilla, she thinks. Finally, she breaks down and asks the guy is that vanilla she smells, because he's the kind of guy she can just talk to about any old thing, and the guy gets all embarrassed. He tells her the odor is coming from him, because his family owned a pickle factory, so his hands usually smelled of vinegar and pickling salts and garlic and whatnot, not very romantic stuff, and his dad had told him that when he had a date with a girl he really liked, he should soak his hands after work in warm milk and vanilla. It was the only thing that could kill the pickle smell, plus the milk would make your hands softer, his dad had told him, in the event you should be lucky enough that the girl lets you touch her.

The guy is explaining all this to the woman, and for

some reason suddenly the tears are pouring over my bottom lids and streaming down my face, down my neck, into my collar. I don't remember what happened in the movie after that, or how it ended.

What I remember is crying that night in my chair, even letting myself make noises out loud, outside of my body. Crying harder than I did when our first dog, Buck, had the run-in with the porcupine and we had to put him down the day after Boxing Day. Harder than I cried the morning Ally left town in the passenger seat of Mitch Sawyer's new truck. They left Mitch with the minivan, for the kids. I cried harder and longer and louder than ever.

I woke up with what felt like sand in my eyes, still in the armchair, with the coloured bars on the TV glowing and humming in the dark. I lifted the lid on the cello to look at it, then latched it shut, and went straight to bed.

I dreamt of nothing, and woke up an hour before my alarm went off. I washed the lone coffee cup in the sink, noting that it meant I hadn't eaten anything at all for dinner the night before, shaved three days off my face, and took Buck Buck for an extra long walk before we headed to the shop. I even managed to beat Franco there, which he hated. Franco could sit sometimes for an hour and a half in the office in the morning without lifting a finger to get anything actually accomplished, but as long as he got there before I did, he figured he was still showing me what work looked like. I wouldn't mind so much if he made better coffee.

I put on a pot of strong stuff, swept the floor, and read almost the entire paper before it was time to plug in the open sign. Franco showed up just before seven-thirty, clean-shaven and reeking of cologne still, a sure sign he had gone out to the bar last night after broomball and got drunk, or lucky, or maybe both.

He started in before the bells on the front door had even stopped jingling.

"You're early. Hey, you know that substitute teacher from the French school? The one from Montreal? Ten minutes ago she was sitting in my lap, feeding me fruit with her fingers. What a night."

I flipped the page on my newspaper. Said nothing.

He stared through his eyebrows at me, and made for the coffee pot. "You look tired. Hungover? Jesus, Joey, I could polish my boots with this. Look, there's oil floating around on top of the coffee you made."

"It just has some kick to it."

"You look like you need it."

"I'm fine."

"I'm just asking, Joey."

"What, Franco? What are you asking me? You're not even making sense."

"Jesus, your mother was right. You *are* a miserable bastard. A guy can't even ask how his coworker is feeling around here these days without you getting paranoid."

"You were talking to my mom about me? She called me a bastard?"

"See what I mean?" Franco took a big gulp of his coffee. "Well, I'm going to work. Can't sit around all day reading the newspaper."

I lit a cigarette to keep my hands from tossing the phone book at him. The weird thing about Franco is, the only thing that bugs me more than his non-stop talking is when he stops.

I got two tune-ups, a timing chain, and a set of rear breaks done before I even thought about lunch. My mind couldn't keep up with itself, and I needed something to do with my hands, so I could think.

I wasn't one of those guys who would have had a problem with my wife going back to school, was I? Why would she keep something like that a secret? She must have actually hid it from me, too, the mail from the university, things like that. Where the fuck had I been? Sleeping with Kathleen was something I could see Ally neglecting to mention, but long-distance education?

I thought about calling her and asking, but that would unlock the other five thousand questions that had been banging on the insides of my eyelids for the last twelve months and thirteen days since she left.

I couldn't ask her about school without asking her why she never told me about Kathleen. Without asking if she was lying when she dreamed about the bees and me and the farm just outside of town, or if she ever missed me. If they ever did it in our bed, under the quilt my mom gave me and that her mom gave her. Stuff like that. Stuff I didn't know, couldn't ask, couldn't know but couldn't help wondering about.

It looked to me like this question was going to have to join the rest of them and become just another one of Allyson's secrets.

The thought of it all made me want to smoke.

Franco was in the office boiling water to make Cup-a-Soup and whispering into the phone to the French teacher, from the sounds of it.

"Give me a bit to go home and clean up. I'll call you when I'm leaving my place, okay? I'll bring the wine." He hung up and eyed me while I lit a cigarette.

"You look like shit. Why don't you take the afternoon off, get out of here for a while? You've already worked us right out of anything else to do today. I can close up."

"I thought you had a date tonight?"

"Not till eight o'clock or so. I can't get there too early. I have to pace myself, she's half my age."

Franco patted his gut and grinned. "Go home, Joey. Go play your new violin. Have a beer. Jerk off. Whatever you do."

"It's a cello, Franco."

"Whatever. Go play it. You're driving me nuts. Come

back on Monday, when you've lightened the fuck up a bit."

"Since when do you listen to my mother?"

"Since you're about as fun to work with as a hot rash on my ass. Since your mother is right. Take three days. Take a drive. Take a load off. Get a haircut. Get laid. Get over yourself. Something."

I sighed. "Thanks, Franco."

"Don't thank me. I'm doing this for myself. And for your mother. She thinks you need counselling. Or Prozac."

"Prozac? Fuck me. My own mother said I need pills? What'd you say to that?"

"I said I'd see about talking you into taking a long weekend. I'll call you if I need you."

I took off my coveralls, hung them up, and called the dog.

It seemed weird to be at home during the day. Middle of the week. No leaf blowers, no kids playing ball hockey in the street. Nothing but Oprah on, and the bald guy.

I took a shower, scrubbed the grease from the cracks in my hands, under my nails. Engine oil probably wasn't great for cellos. I removed the instrument from its case, taking care not to bang it on the coffee table. I ran my index finger up and down the strings which whistled, hollow and mellow. I sat one cheek on the edge of the big chair and pulled the little stand thing out of the bottom of the cello. I pressed the middle finger of my left hand onto a string, thinking of this rockabilly band I had seen once at the North County Fair, and plonked the string with my other thumb. The cello hummed alive between my legs. Buck Buck growl-barked once, then circled around a couple of times before laying down beside me.

It only took ten minutes or so before the tips of my fin-

26

gers started throbbing. I needed to get up and cut the nail on my ring finger shorter so I could press the strings down with it properly. I leaned the cello up against my chair, but when I went to get up, Buck Buck wagged his tail at me and thumped the cello, which then started to slide down the arm of the chair. I snatched it by the neck and then carried it like a sleeping kid, safely placing it into its case. I would have to be more careful with the thing. It wasn't an electric guitar.

On the way to the bathroom for the nail clippers, I caught a look at myself in the mirror. Franco was right. I did look tired. Blue bags under my eyes, and I needed a haircut. You could really see the grey. And the sink needed cleaning. The toilet, too, upon further inspection. The place was falling into disrepair. I didn't want a bathroom like Franco's, or Rick Davis's since his wife Anna left. I dug around under the sink for some cleaner and a rag. I actually put a new roll of paper right onto the holder thing, and threw out two empty shampoo bottles. My wedding ring was sitting next to the sink. It was stuck there in a pool of dried soap leftovers, and when I picked it up and put it in the cabinet, it left a silvery green shadow where it had been sitting on the ceramic. I cut my nails, then collected up the dirty towels and went to go find the vacuum.

A couple of hours later I had cleaned the house, done three loads of laundry, and taken out the garbage and recycling. I took Buck Buck for a walk, heading down Eighth Avenue towards the Red Deer River. I could see a line of twenty or thirty sets of headlights on the highway, all going north out of downtown. I looked at my watch. Five o'clock, right on the nose.

I was hungry.

27

I ran into Marion Bradley, the librarian, in the cereal aisle at the Food Fair. She was wearing a dark red sweater and lipstick, so she looked a lot different than she did at work. I almost didn't recognize her.

"Well, hello there, you," she smiled. "I was just thinking I needed to call you about bringing my car in. Swap the snow tires on. Get a tune-up."

I nodded, hoping she wasn't looking into my cart. Cans of soup, cereal. Pathetic. I needed to cook more. "I was going to stop by the library this week, too." I took a couple cans of kidney beans off the shelf and put them in my cart. Maybe I would make chili. I could make chili. "I need to see if you've got any books on how to play the cello."

"Ally is taking up the cello? Is there anything your wife cannot do?"

I coughed, thought for a second.

"Uh, no. It's for me. I'm learning. Well, teaching myself, at least I'm trying to, that's why I need a book."

"That's totally great, Joey. Come by. I'll find you a cello book, or we'll order you one from Calgary. Do you and Ally jam together now? She plays the clarinet, right?"

"The oboe."

"Right, the oboe. I've always thought it would be great to jam with people. I wish I played something. Do you do duets?"

"Ally moved to Calgary. I guess nobody told you. We split up. She doesn't know I'm playing the cello."

Marion's face pinked up. "I'm so sorry, Joey, I didn't know. I'm sorry."

This was the part I hated. All the I'm-sorrys and the how-are-you-doings and the you-should-come-by-for-dinners. What do you say to them all?

"I'm sorry, too."

Marion stared at her shoes, then at mine. "Come by the library, and we'll find you your cello book. You take care of yourself."

Oh, yeah, and the you-take-care-of-yourselfs. I didn't like those much, either.

One thing I had definitely discovered since Ally had left was that there were two distinct kinds of heartbreak I had to deal with: there was the private kind, and I guess I could pretty much deal with that, and then there was the more public version, the kind of shared tragedy that I found could really kick a guy in the ribs, because it could just sneak up on you like that, right there in the supermarket, when you were occupied trying to think about what to get for dinner.

I was halfway through my soup and sandwich when someone knocked on the back door. Must be someone I knew. It was Rick Davis, holding five cold Canadians, still in their plastic rings, a slim black plastic case tucked under one arm.

"Buddy." He pushed past me into the kitchen. "What's up? I tried to phone first, but nobody picked up."

"Why'd you come over then, if you thought I wasn't home?"

"I said nobody answered. Didn't say I thought you weren't home. Aren't you going to ask me what's in the case?"

"What's in the case, Davey?"

"It's a .22 pistol, nickel-plated, holds eight rounds. I need to empty these cans, so I can try it out on something. I thought you could help me out."

He twisted a beer out of its plastic ring for me, and I popped the tab. I motioned for him to have a seat. He left his boots on, and flipped a chair around to sit on.

"It looks pretty good in here. You clean up or something? Is that a new stove?"

I nodded, and grabbed an ashtray for the table. Rick Davis was famous for talking with a two- inch ash hanging from his fingers, and I had just mopped the floor.

"Franco tells me you're taking up the upright bass?"

"It's a cello."

"Fancy. So how's the cello, then? Wanna play me a few movements? I told Franco you were smarter than we all think, taking up a classy instrument like that. Any dumb fuck can play 'Stairway to Heaven' on the electric guitar. But a classical type of deal, now that's bound to attract a higher class of woman."

"I'm not learning the cello to meet chicks, Davis. My mom is on my case to get a new hobby. It's either that, or Prozac, apparently."

"Your sister, too."

"What's that?"

"Sarah. She dropped by the job site. The gym floor, in the new school, me and Smiley got that contract. Keep us busy till after Christmas, that job. As long as I can keep Smiley and Jimmy Peel, the general contractor, from ripping each other a new one. Man, those two. Like fucking oil and water. I can never tell who started it with them. Stresses me out, too, being always caught in the middle. Pissing contest. You got any rolling papers?"

"The drawer beside the fridge. Anyways, what did Sarah want?"

"Well, she came by work a couple of days ago, asking if I'd seen much of you lately, how did you seem, if I could take you hunting or something, get you out of the house, shit like that."

"Those two are the ones who need a new hobby. Mom and Sarah obviously have too much time on their hands."

"Just do us both a favour then, Joey, and come and shoot some holes in some beer cans with me. I'll tell your sister that you seem just fine, and they'll be off both our cases."

"I am fine. I'd be better if everyone and their fucking dog wasn't asking me how I was doing all the time."

"I hear you, partner. But that's the way it goes. Same thing happened when Anna and I first split up, remember? Matter of fact, if I do recall correctly, you came by my place with a six-pack to give me the speech that one night."

"Your dad talked me into that. But that's because you were drinking."

"Of course I was drinking. She took me to the cleaners. Thought I was gonna have to sell the business for a while there."

Everybody knew that Rick had almost lost his business because of the booze, not so much the divorce, but you couldn't say a thing like that to him. He'd got things pretty much back under control now anyway, so what would be the point? No one wants the whole truth about themselves all the time anyway.

Rick ran his tongue along a perfectly rolled joint and twisted one end into a point. He ripped a small corner off the rolling paper pack, rolled it into a tiny spiral, and slipped it into the other end of the doobie, to make a filter. "You wanna step into the garage with me?"

"I'll come with you, but I don't think I'll smoke any. I'll be crashed out by nine-thirty if I do."

"No early night for you, buddy, I promised I'd make you get out of the house for a while. We're going to the Capitol for a game of pool. There's a bluegrass band in town. Steel guitar, the whole shebang. Put on a clean shirt. Franco's bringing his French teacher and a couple of her girlfriends. French-Canadian tree planters. Nothing like a new pair of hands creeping up the front of your Levi's, like Franco always says."

"Franco talks too much."

"True enough, but every once in a while he's right. That's what finally got me to smarten up, remember? The front desk girl from the Westmark? The twelve-stepper?"

"The vegan? I thought she drove you crazy."

"Well, I never said it was a match made in heaven, but still, she buttered my toast for a couple of months and it helped snap me out of it."

"I don't need to snap out of anything, Davis. I'm fine."

"According to you. But your sister and your mother and Franco think you're a grouchy bastard who only eats canned soup."

"Franco talks too much."

"You already said that." Rick lit the joint, right there in the kitchen. "Go change your shirt."

I cracked open the window and pushed the ashtray across the table to him. "I thought you were gonna smoke that thing in the garage?"

"Jesus, they're right. You *are* uptight."

"I just cleaned the whole house, you're here for ten minutes and now it smells like a youth hostel."

"Let's go get your wick dipped, my friend. You are one high-strung individual."

I let my shoulders drop and sighed. "One beer. And you leave the handgun here."

"Whatever, Oscar. I'm driving."

The parking lot outside the Capitol was packed, mostly muddy pick-ups and SUVs. It was only Thursday night. It seemed like forever since I had been to the bar. Ally hated bars. Said they didn't foster conversation. She wasn't much of a drinker, either. Just red wine. I only saw her drunk once or twice, at dinner parties.

There was a cluster of folks smoking outside the front doors, huddled on the sidewalk, blowing into cupped hands and breathing little clouds of steam and smoke into the cold. I forgot about the smoking ban. It had been that long since I had been out drinking. Smokeless bars in Alberta. Weird.

Franco and his threesome pulled up chairs for us. Marianne, Charlotte, and Sophie. Sophie was kind of cute, drinking vodka and cranberry, and smelling woodsy. White white teeth. Marianne was obviously the French teacher, as she seemed to be the one paying close attention to Franco, who was holding court, Labatt's sceptre in hand.

"Here we go, Joey and Rick, Rick and Joey." He motioned to the waitress, who sidled towards the table, a tray full of empties and ashtrays balanced on one hip.

She leaned over and gave the table a healthy shot of her cleavage. "What can I get you fellas? Another round for you too, Franco?"

We ordered and she disappeared with Rick's credit card. Apparently being the recently divorced guy meant I didn't have to pay for my drinks. Maybe my mom was right about silver linings.

"Joey can tell what's wrong with an engine just by giving it a listen," Franco told the girls. "That's what's gonna make him a good musician, I bet. The ears."

I could suddenly feel my ears glowing red and hot. This was the part where everybody tried to introduce me to any single woman in the vicinity. It was no wonder I didn't ever feel like going out. I sat through a pitcher, watched Franco and Rick lose a game of pool to Marianne and Charlotte, made enough small talk with Sophie to not seem rude, and hopped in a cab alone around ten-thirty. It was raining almost snow, and the wind had picked up.

Buck Buck pounded the tiles in the kitchen with his tail when I came through the door like I'd been gone for a week. I scratched him behind the ears for a while, then turned on the television and crossed my fingers for a good movie to be on.

Then the power went out. Streetlights, too. I opened the curtains all the way to let a bit of moon in, turned on the gas fireplace, and lit the candles on the coffee table. Allyson used to love it when the power went out. I hauled the cello out of its case, pulling its wide torso up close to my face. I liked the smell of it. Wax and wood and something coppery, like an old penny. I picked out a tune in the dark with my fingertips. I hadn't figured out the bow yet, so I kind of plucked away like it was an overweight guitar. The first little bit of "I Found My Thrill on Blueberry Hill." Not exactly a sonata, just the first thing that came into my head. The cab driver had been playing it in the car on the way home. CKRW. All the oldies, all the time.

My dad used to sing that song to my mom when I was a kid. They would dance in the kitchen, him in his grey work pants, my mom giggling, her slippers whispering against the linoleum. I always did like that song.

I spent the rest of that weekend eating, sleeping, cleaning, and screwing around on the cello. I raked the leaves off the yard and the boulevard, drained the gas out of the mower, and cleaned the gutters. I made a big pot of chili, and learned to make a wheezy but recognizable note with the bow instead of just my thumb, which was raw on the one side. I played some Beatles records really loud, played with the dog, played with myself. I had a good time.

I went to work Monday with a new haircut and some semblance of a new attitude. Cranked up some Frank Zappa in the shop instead of news radio. Took Franco out to lunch.

I had my head under the dash of a Ford Tempo installing a new wiper relay when Franco tapped my knee.

"Telephone, Joey. It's Jim Carson. The cello-man."

I took the cordless from him.

"Hullo, Jim."

"That you, Joey? It's Jim Carson here, out at Archie's. I'm calling because the car I bought from you broke down. Can't get it started, and I can't figure out why. Had one of Archie's boys take a look too, no dice. I was wondering if you could come around and have a look for me, see what's up?"

"Sure, Jim, sure. I'm sure it's nothing major. Like I said, I gave it the once-over before I put it up for sale, but I'll come check it out. You around tomorrow morning? I have to take the oil to the recyclers, I'll be driving right past your place."

35

"I was hoping you could come sooner than that. I bought the car to get out of town. I was supposed to leave this morning, but the car quit running. Won't even turn over, and I'm supposed to be on my way already."

"Righto, Jim. Sorry about that. I'll come around in an hour."

I told Franco I was going to run a few errands, and threw some tools in the truck. I felt kind of bad. There had been nothing wrong with the Volvo a week ago. I'd fix it up for Jim right away, because I didn't want him asking me for the cello back. There was something about it. I'd have to ask Jim if he had any tips. Like how to make it not sound like I was dragging a cat backwards across a countertop, for instance.

Jim Carson lived in the southwest end of Archie Lang's old place, the second driveway past the road that headed up to Archie's big farmhouse. I turned right on a rutted dirt road that ran alongside a power line and into a small gravel lot containing an equipment shed, a corrugated tin pump house, and Carson's yellow bus. The Volvo was parked in the long grass just on the other side of a neat row of firewood. Smoke billowed into the grey sky from the small chimney at the back of the bus. I wondered how much it would cost to insure that thing with a woodstove in it, although it didn't look like the bus had moved since the cowboy had parked it three years ago, the tires being swallowed up by horsetails.

I parked my truck and knocked on the bus's accordion door. Buck Buck took off into the field after a gopher. Jim slid the door open and stood at the top of the stairs. "Keys are in it. I'll put on a pot of coffee."

Like I said before, he got right to business, that guy.

Didn't even ask me in. I grabbed my toolbox and a canvas tarp out of the back of my truck, which I laid out on the grass, and then got into the car. I turned the key. It tried to turn over, whining and audibly draining the battery. Looked like he had tried to start it for a while, and run it down. I could smell gas. Flooded it, too.

I sat back in the seat for a minute. That's when I noticed it. The soot. A thin film of fine black soot covered the entire interior of the car. It showed where I slid my finger along the dash, was already all over my palms. Then, underneath the gas, I smelled the tang of exhaust. Maybe he had a leak in the exhaust system, or a blockage in the muffler.

I popped the hood and got out of the car. Took the trouble light out of my toolbox. There was still enough juice in the battery to turn the engine over, maybe it had dirty plugs, or the flywheel was going on it.

I unlocked the trunk to grab the jack I had left in there when I sold the car. Lying next to the spare and the jack and the tire iron was a brand new roll of duct-tape and a coil of four-inch plastic tubing. It took me a minute, but then it all started clicking in my head. The soot. The hose. The tape. The smell of exhaust. The cowboy was in a hurry to leave, he had said.

My right hand reached automatically for the pack of smokes in the left chest pocket of my coat. I lit one with suddenly very cold hands. The cowboy had tried to commit suicide, but his exit had been thwarted by the fact that the car I had given him had ceased to run long enough for him to kill himself with. The man in the bus would be dead already, had he not traded me for a lemon of a used car.

I jacked up the Volvo so I could have a better look underneath. Slid my tarp underneath, and slid myself onto it.

I wasn't so much looking for what was wrong with the car as I was trying to figure out what I was going to say to Jim Carson. Should I let him know I had stumbled upon what he had been trying to do? What if I was wrong? Fixing cars was what I did, what I had always done, but how could I fix this one, just so he could off himself in it? I could just give him back the cello and tow the car straight back to the shop, but that wouldn't fix whatever it was that was wrong with Jim Carson. I had never shown much talent when it came to fixing people. I decided to stall a bit, tell him I was going to have to order some parts or something, and think on it all overnight. I let out my breath. I hadn't realized I'd been holding it.

I packed up my tools, put them back into the truck, and knocked on the bus door again. He opened it right away, like he'd been standing right behind it. Handed me a steaming cup of black coffee.

He had two sugar cubes in one hand. Raised an eyebrow. Did I want some?

I nodded and he tossed them into my coffee.

"You figure it out?"

I took a sip, burned the roof of my mouth. Stovetop coffee. My favourite kind.

"Looks to me like it's something in your exhaust system. For sure you need a new muffler. Need to get it up on the hoist to be sure. You didn't put that cheap Super Save gas in it, did you? I see all kinds of fuel line troubles from bad gas. Maybe a fuel pump, hard to say."

Jim showed the lines in his forehead. "I filled it up yesterday at Mitch Sawyer's place. I never buy cheap gas. How long to fix it, you think? You got the parts?"

I shook my head. "Not in stock. Have to call Nelson's

Auto, see if they've got any old Volvos on the lot, if not I'll have to call the dealership in Calgary. That's the only problem with those cars. Parts. I'll take care of it, though, whatever it is."

His face darkened. He shifted his weight to his other foot, scratched his stubble. "How long, you reckon?"

I didn't dare ask him why he was in such a rush to asphyxiate himself. How would you approach something like that? I barely knew the guy.

"Depends on what I'm gonna need. I'll tow it back to the shop right now, let you know when I track down the parts. Maybe tomorrow, maybe the day after. Let me check around, I'll call you in an hour?"

"I don't have a phone. I had to walk down to the Esso to call you this morning."

"Can I leave a message for you with Archie?"

He shook his head. "We try to stay out of each other's way as much as possible."

"Right. Then I'll just bring the car out when I've got it running again. It's on me, Jim. Sorry for the hassle."

It wasn't until I got back to the shop that I realized I never asked Jim Carson if he even played the cello. Just as well, I figured. He obviously had other things on his mind.

I gave Whit Nelson a call as soon as I got back to the shop and backed the car into the service bay. Whit had been shutting his salvage lot down early from time to time lately, and I didn't want to miss him. Ricardo, Whit's right-hand guy, was taking time off because his wife just had twins, and Whit himself was slowing down. I'd even heard it rumoured around he was thinking of selling his place, and that they were going to clear the lot and the old house behind it and build a Wal-Mart or something. That maybe Whit was going to retire out to him and Lily's little place on Cub Lake. I'd have to drive to the A-1 Salvage out at the cutoff if Whit ever shut his place down, and I never liked either one of the brothers that ran that place. Whit got his nephew to check the lot for a used muffler, while Whit and I talked how's business for a bit. I tried not to think too much about repairing Jim Carson's car considering what he needed it fixed so bad for, but didn't know what else I could do with a broken car except fix it. The nephew came back after a minute to say they had one, and Whit sent him back out to pull it for me, and invited me into the office for tea.

I used to love coming out to Nelson's Salvage for parts with my dad, ever since I was a little kid and my feet couldn't touch the floor of the cab in the old flatbed. Whit and my dad would always sit around and shoot the shit for a while before any business got done, drinking orange pekoe tea with canned milk and Roger's sugar cubes out of the box, as was Whit's way. He didn't believe in coffee, never touched the stuff. Didn't believe in exchanging money without sitting down for a cup of tea first, either. The kettle was always warm on the back burner of the stove in the tiny lunchroom behind the front counter. Sometimes he'd let me fool around with the forklift in the warehouse, a couple of times he even put a car in the crusher, just for us to watch. Lily, his vastly bosomed wife, kept a supply of cookies or macaroons in a tin on the Formica table, next to the pile of old car magazines.

The cookie supply dried up a few years ago, after Whit's heart attack and the cholesterol alerts, and the sugar cubes became little pink packets of Sweet 'n Low, but the kettle was still on. He had Frank Sinatra playing on the greasy transistor radio on the shelf behind the register, and the floor smelled freshly waxed.

"It's good to see you, Joey. How's your mother? Help yourself, I've just made a pot of fresh."

I hadn't seen Whit for more than three months. He looked older, the long bones showing through the skin on the back of his hands, water in his eyes. He leaned on a worn rubber-tipped cane. The only time I'd ever seen him use it before was when he was walking around downtown.

"Use the blue mug, it's clean. I already got myself some tea in my thermal cup here. You got yourself one of these yet? The granddaughter got me mine, from the Starbucks. Made by Nissan, believe it or not, but they sure keep your drink hot. Did I ask you already how was your mother? Lily has been missing bingo since her wrists have been acting up, and I've lost my news source."

"She's good, Whit. Busy as ever. Nothing seems to slow her down."

"It's that new beau of hers, that'll do it."

I sipped my tea, looking at his face to see if he was pulling my leg. "My mom has a boyfriend? Where did you hear that?"

"Lily, who else. You didn't know? She told me about it couple months back. Quite the stir it was making with the old birds at bingo, I guess. The guy is loaded, apparently, owns the new golf course. Used to be a lawyer type, for an exploration outfit out of Edmonton, I think it was. I met the guy, seems a nice enough sort. Lily thinks he's dead handsome. He came by looking for something or other for that '59 Ford of his. Nice truck. All stock."

"The robin's egg and white one?"

He nodded. "The very same."

"My mom hasn't said anything to me." I shook my head. "The guy with the goatee? Always on his cell phone?"

"I didn't notice that. But he didn't stay for tea. Lots of folks don't anymore, though."

"I stood in line next to him at the liquor store two weeks ago. He could have been buying wine my mother drank. Nobody tells me anything."

"I'm telling you, aren't I? Maybe your mother thinks you won't approve. But it's been four years your dad's been gone now, Joey. You should be happy for her, a little this and that, it'll keep her young." Whit winked, then coughed, hollow in the back of his throat.

"I'll be happy for her as soon as I'm over being shocked. Isn't he a bit young for her?"

"Five years, I think Lily said. And filthy rich and good-looking. No wonder the old tongues are wagging."

"Good for her, then," I said. Then I wondered if my mom had told Franco. Sarah knew, no doubt.

Whit looked at his watch and cleared his throat. "I'm going to have to run, Joey. I got the nephew to haul the part around to the side door for you. Lily has a roast in the oven."

The sun was going down as I drove back up the highway towards the shop, making the frost on the grass beside the highway glow orange. I would have to fire up the furnace in the shop tonight, so I could work late. I was going to fix the cowboy's car tonight, and tow it straight out there tomorrow morning. In the meantime, I had to figure out what the fuck I was going to say to the guy when I gave him back his car. I could hardly tell him I hoped it was going to run fine from now on.

I even wondered for a minute if the guy had been kind of ass-backwardly asking me for help. He hadn't made much of an attempt to hide the signs very well. I thought about asking my mom or Franco what they would do, but I didn't want to spill the guy's private life all over town. Those two, running their own public address system, it seemed to me. I never ever thought of killing myself before, even when I was a teenager, but I imagined if I did, I'd want to be kind of private about it. Wouldn't want someone bringing it up in the Food Fair or something. I figured the best thing I could do with the cowboy's little secret was to keep it to myself.

Three hours and two cups of coffee later, I got the Volvo to turn over. I parked it outside, locked up, and went home.

I towed the car back out to Archie's with the new flatbed truck first thing the next day. It had been purchased by my father almost nine years ago, but it was still called the new flatbed for some reason, mostly because it wasn't the old flatbed. When I first pulled up into the gravel lot, I noticed there was no smoke coming from the bus. Then I saw Archie's blue pick-up. The cowboy had said him and Archie tried to stay out of each other's way, but there was the old landlord himself, loading the neat stack of firewood into the box of his truck. My heart thumped behind my undershirt. Maybe the cowboy had tried another method. I jumped out of my truck, my boots crunching cold gravel.

"Hey, Joe. What brings you out here?"

"Got this car fixed for Jim Carson. He around? In the bus?"

"You missed him by about an hour. He just left."

"Did he say when he'd be back?"

"I hope never. Told him three years ago he could stay for a month. Was a friend of my wife's when they were kids, I only did it as a favour to her. She woulda wanted me to, had a thing for strays, may she rest in peace, but I'm still feeding her remaining four cats. I hate the critters."

"He left for good? Without his car? He said he needed it fixed right away. I only picked it up yesterday afternoon. Don't you think that's weird?"

"Tell me one thing about that fella that isn't strange, I dare you to. I never took to him. He woulda been gone a long time ago, except he kept so much to himself, I could never come up with a good enough reason to get rid of him. Kept an eye on the water pump for me, never came knocking for anything. Not too pleased he's left this eyesore of a bus behind, though, but he did leave me two hundred bucks to have it towed, or for my trouble if I manage to sell it to someone. You need an old school bus, Joey?"

I shook my head. "Did he mention where he was headed, Archie? Leave an address? I guess I'll need to call him about the car, since it's his by law, he filled out the transfer papers and all."

"He left on foot. Barely even thanked me. Didn't ask

45

him where he was headed cuz I couldn't much care. You best turn around and take that car back with you too, or it'll end up one more thing I have to do, if I know how these things tend to go."

"He left town on foot? What about his stuff?"

"Guy never seemed to have much. Books, mostly. He left with one duffel bag and an old guitar case."

"Mind if I take a look in the bus?"

"Knock yourself out, Joey. And give your mother my regards. Is she gonna marry that lawyer of hers, or just run around town with him?"

Fuck me, I thought. Even Archie knows.

The bus smelled of wood smoke, and that must-and-rust vinyl tang of old vehicles. The smell that meant happy to me if the sun was shining, and something else altogether when it wasn't.

All of the passenger seats had been removed, save for the one behind the driver's, and the floor had been re-covered with tongue and groove plywood, stained a mahogany colour, and then varnished. There was a tiny one-legged table, one edge screwed into a two-by-four attached to the wall of the bus. A woodstove, a box for kindling, and newspapers beside it. One chair. A single bunk, its spare foam mattress stripped of blankets or sheets. A bowl-shaped sink in a three-foot wide countertop, shelves with no doors underneath, and a two-burner Coleman stove. A label-less tin can beside the sink contained one knife, one fork, one teaspoon, one soup spoon, and a spatula. A bookshelf above the bunk, empty now save for a box of matches. The faded curtains that covered the bus's windows facing Archie's house were all pulled shut. The ones on the windows opposite were tied back, revealing the close-cropped hayfield outside. The cowboy had boxed in a small garden between the bus and the field, four two-by-tens on their sides nailed together in a tidy rectangle. The garden had been harvested, and the soil turned and raked for winter. A frost-weary squash plant soldiered on, lonely inside an old tire planter beside the empty vegetable patch.

The guy obviously wasn't long on luxury. Sparse was the first word that came to mind. No wonder he hadn't invited me in for coffee. He only owned the one chair. The cowboy had walked off with just a duffel bag, according to Archie, yet had left almost nothing behind.

I noticed what looked like a couple of maps, folded up and clothes-pinned to the sun visor above the driver's seat. I pulled them out, curious. I wondered where this old bus had travelled, before the cowboy parked it here. There was a map of Western Canada, the kind that shows you where the rest areas and showers and campgrounds are, one of Alberta logging roads, and a street map of Calgary. There was a round compass suction-cupped just below the rear-view mirror, a cup holder, and a little storage compartment behind the handle that opened the bus door. Inside it, I found a water-stained repair manual elastic-banded with the registration papers, and a little book that said "Service, Repair and Mileage Records." I opened it. I'm a mechanic. You can tell a lot about a guy by how he treats his engine. I told my sister this before she married Jean-Paul, but she wouldn't listen.

Jim Carson had changed the oil in the bus every five thousand clicks, since he started keeping records anyway, which was twenty years ago, according to his tidy script. The bus had been getting approximately twelve miles to the gallon of high-octane gas when it was parked, not bad for an old beast like this. I liked a man who put high octane in an old vehicle. Showed a little foresight, my dad used to say. I wondered if the motor would turn over. Looked like the cowboy had taken care of it. The keys were under the visor.

The driver's seat squeaked cold air under my cheeks when I sat down. The keys were on a leather keychain, shaped like a totem pole with the words "Pemberton Towing" on it. No other keys, just the ignition and the little silver one for the gas cap. Archie's tail lights were now disappearing down the road in the dust. He wouldn't care if I fired it up.

The engine turned over a little reluctantly, but caught and coughed to life. Once it warmed up a little, it sounded all right. I rubbed my palm on the shiny grip of the gearshift. The metal of the clutch arm had worn through the rubber foot-pedal. There was something on the floor, a little corner of white paper peeking out from under the Bluebird floor mat.

A postcard. I turned the ignition off, and the bus grumbled into silence.

I picked the postcard up, feeling a bit like Lenny from *Law and Order*, when the clue music starts up. The picture side was a shot of Drumheller's Largest Dinosaur in the World sculpture. I hated that thing. You could buy a postcard just like this one in every gas station and corner store in town. Not much of a clue.

The other side contained two lines, thin blue stand-up script, same as the handwriting in the bus's records. Jim had written a postcard to someone and never mailed it. *Dear Cecelia, Seth, Isaac, and Lady: Thought the boys might like this. Things are fine, and I'll see you for Christmas, love Jim.*

It was addressed to a Cecilia Carson in Calgary. This sleuth business was easier than I thought. Sounded like he had an ex-wife and a couple of kids, young ones, probably, less than two hours away. I would call directory assistance, leave a message with her. Let him know his car was fixed, and then at least I could say I had kept good on my half of our deal.

My big plan ground to a halt about half an hour later back at the shop, when directory assistance informed me that there was no listing for a C or a Cecelia Carson anywhere in the Calgary area. I checked the postcard, which I had folded and tucked into my pocket next to my smokes. There was no date on it. Who knew how long it had been sliding around on the floor of the bus? Maybe Cecelia and the kids had moved years ago.

I took out the company chequebook from the bottom drawer of my desk and paid all the bills in the inbox on the counter. Checked the shop schedule next to the phone, and the work orders on the clipboard. It looked like we weren't busy for the rest of this week. Always slow this time of year, after the snow tires go on and the fall tune-ups are over with. Franco was rotating the tires on a Saturn in the service bay. I brought him a cup of coffee, one sugar with Coffee-mate, just how he liked it.

"What do you want?" He took off his work gloves. He always wore gloves when he worked. My dad used to give him a hard time about it, how he would slather his paws with the hand cleaner that had lanolin in it every morning, and then squeeze them into buckskin work gloves. "I like to caress a woman, not sandpaper the skin off her," Franco would say, showing his teeth.

"You mind if I take off for a couple of days? Things are slow enough, should be fine with just the one guy."

Franco gave me a look as he sipped his coffee. "Take

as much time as you want, I'll be fine here. I could always call the kid in if things got busy." The kid was Jerry Collins' oldest boy, Nicolas. He worked for us the last two summers, part-time here and part-time at the RV car wash next door. Good kid. Nick could give Franco a hand if something came up.

"Going hunting with Davis?"

I shook my head. "Into the city. I need to take Allyson the last of her stuff."

Franco stared at me.

"And I'm going to look into finding a cello teacher."

He raised his eyebrows. "Still got that thing? Thought maybe you traded it back when you towed the Volvo in here again."

"Carson left town this morning without taking his car with him, and Archie wouldn't let me leave it on his property. Didn't even tell me he was leaving, or what he wanted me to do with the car."

"I told you that guy was weird. Law says if he abandons the car for more than thirty days without paying the bill, it belongs to the shop that fixed it. Then you got yourself a car and a cello. Good deal for you."

"Except I told Jim I would pay the bill for the repair, because I felt bad it broke down on him so soon. Wonder what the lawyers would have to say about that?"

"Common sense would say the guy didn't want the car, so he left it with the guy he got it from. I figure if he left the papers in the glove box, it's yours. You going to Calgary alone then?"

I nodded. "I'm even going to see if my mom can take the dog, since I can't fit him and the cello into the cab of the truck at the same time."

"As long as you don't leave the beast with me. Last time he shed all over my suede couch. That dog never liked me. Go, Joey, have a good time. Buy yourself something new. Get into a bit of trouble. Find yourself a friendly cello teacher, maybe learn a few other things."

I had been imagining the cello teacher looking like a matronly older lady, with spectacles and grandchildren. But what did I know? I was the only guy with a cello I knew. I'd have to stop by the library on my way out of town, get an instruction book. Say hi to Marion. It had been a long time since I'd been out of Drumheller alone. Since before Allyson and I got married. Maybe I'd even buy a new CD for the road.

My mom came to the door with a tea towel in her hand. The smell of bread in the oven wafted past her and mixed with the chill I brought in with me. It was starting to smell like it could snow.

"Joseph. It's nice to see you. You want some fresh bread with raspberry jam?" Then she narrowed her eyes at me. "How come you're not at the shop? Everything okay?"

"It's slow. I'm taking off into the city for a couple of days. I packed up the rest of Ally's stuff. I'm going to save her the postage and drive it into Calgary."

"That's very kind of you. I know Allyson has been busy, and money is tight with her school. I talked to her the day before yesterday, and we both agree it's best if you two take care of things."

Was there anybody in Alberta that my mother hadn't talked to recently?

"I know, Mom, I'm already doing it."

She passed me a plate with a thick slice of hot bread and jam on it.

"Don't I-know-Mom me, you. That reminds me. I have to hear from Franco my own son is playing the viola?"

"It's a cello, Mom. I only got it last week. And while we're on the subject, I have to hear from Whit Nelson that my own mother has a boyfriend? From what I heard, he's not even all that new."

She sat back in her oak chair, one of a set of six that matched the table. Light Oak, to go with the new cork floor, just like Sarah's. Rick Davis was making a fortune off our family's new flooring habits.

"That Lily Nelson never could keep her big yap shut."

"Does Sarah know?"

She didn't answer me. I knew it.

"Why wouldn't you tell me, Mom? It's been four years since Dad. I wouldn't judge you. You're your own person, it's your life. How come you can tell Sarah and not me?"

She stared down at her teacup. "I know you wouldn't judge me, Joseph. You've never been the type. It's just you and your father were so close, I guess I worried you might.... I didn't want you to feel like I would ever stop loving your father. I won't, but I'm learning that I can love someone else, too. That's the God's truth, Joey. I love Jeffrey, he's a very kind man, and we enjoy each other very much. That's the other reason I didn't tell you. I didn't want to step all over your heartbreak with my new romance."

"Just because I'm alone doesn't mean I don't want you to have a friend, mom."

"Jeffrey is more than just a friend."

"You know what I mean, Mom. We don't need to talk about sex."

She drew in her breath, held it for a minute. Gave me

her I'm-going-to-give-you-a-lecture look. I knew that look. My sister had inherited it. My father used to go mow the lawn or something whenever she leveled it on him. I braced myself with a sip of hot tea.

"Joseph, has it ever occurred to you that the reason some people never tell you things is that you don't want to hear them? Getting you to talk about yourself has always been a chore. I don't know where you get it from, because it certainly wasn't me, or your father. We used stay up all night sometimes, the two of us, right here, around the old table, just talking. Solving all the world's problems over a bottle of wine. Your father always stuck up for you, said you were just more private than the rest of us, but I worried it might be something else. Wondered if it was healthy."

She paused, waited to see if I had anything to say in my own defense. I didn't.

"What I'm trying to tell you is it can be hard for a person to open up to you, Joey, and tell you their heart. Talking is a two-way thing. People can't trust their secrets to a guy who doesn't seem to have any of his own."

"How can I have secrets in this family? In this town?"

"I don't mean those kinds of secrets, Joseph. Maybe dreams would be a better word. I've known you for more than forty years, you're my only son, and I've never known what you dream about."

"I used to dream about me and Ally getting a place out of town one day. We talked about having a kid, maybe."

"And then what happened?" She asked me like she already knew the answer, like a grade school teacher might. I studied her face. She knew about my problem, I could tell by how she was looking at me. Ally had spilled it. Ally was the only person in the entire world I had told, except Rick Davis, and I couldn't see Rick talking about my low sperm count to my mother, ever.

"Ally told you about that? I can't believe it. That is my own personal medical information. Why would she have done that?"

"I'm her mother-in-law, Joseph. Her family. I always will be, divorce or not. Her own mother passed when she was so young. We were talking about my grandbaby. Who else would she come to? At first she thought it was her who couldn't...." Her voice trailed off. "Women talk about these kinds of things. She told me how much you wanted a baby."

I sat there for a minute, collecting the breadcrumbs on my plate with my finger. I felt like crying right then and there, at my mother's kitchen table. I remembered those few weeks after the specialist had told me the news, after the million little humiliations inside the tiny room next to his office, the wrinkled girly magazines, the little see-through plastic cup that had Cooper, J. Jr. written on its masking tape label. It was me. Ally had eggs and ovaries, all in working order. I was it. The last Cooper in the line. My sister Sarah and the Broussards would be the end of us.

I watched as a kind of sly grin crept into my mom's face. "No wonder you never got that sleazy Sandra Jennings knocked up in high school. We worried about that, you know."

I laughed. That part was kind of funny.

"I have to admit, Mom, I thought about Sandra, too. All this time I thought I'd just been real lucky real early."

"I never liked her. Neither did your father. She's a

Horseman now. Three little girls, she married that Aaron kid, didn't she? The middle one, with the noisy motorcycle. You should count yourself lucky. She's not as kind on the eyes as she was when you two were little. Hasn't taken care of herself, and it starts to show. Ages a woman earlier than it does men."

I got up and put my plate in the sink. She was starting to get on a roll, and I had stuff to do. I was hitting the road first thing.

"Can I leave Buck Buck with you? Franco has a new girlfriend and can't take him. I'll be back in a couple of days."

"Take as long as you like. He'll be fine. I like the company."

"I thought you had plenty of company lately." I kissed her on the top of her head and half-hugged her. She stood up and turned to lay a full body hug on me. She smelled like lavender, and her bones seemed light in my arms. Mom felt smaller now, and greyer.

"Drive safely, Joseph. Say hello to Ally for me. And Kathy."

"Her name is Kathleen, Mom."

"Kathleen. Well, her, too. Give her my regards."

"I will."

"I like your haircut. You are handsome as ever."

"I'm going now, Mother."

"So go. Take a loaf of bread with you. Make some sandwiches. Mind you, listen to the weather report. It smells like it could snow."

I let myself out the front door, before she got going again with the questions. I tried to sneak out without waking Buck Buck up, but I heard his nails on the hardwood floor as I escaped down the stairs. He sat in the window as I drove away, barking sharply. Then my mom in the window too, shooing him with the tea towel to get down off the couch.

It was still dark when I got up, and there were fingers of frost on my bedroom window, first time that year. I put on my good grey pants and a white shirt, and my leather coat instead of the Stormrider. I didn't know if the cello teacher was going to turn out to look like the matronly grandmother I imagined or Franco's version, but either way, I felt like I should scrub up.

I backed the truck up in front of the garage and loaded Ally's books into the lock box behind the cab. Tossed some clothes into my bag, then hauled the cello out and put it in the passenger seat. It was weird not having the dog underfoot.

I swung into the library parking lot just after eight-thirty. No one in the place at all except an old lady and a pink-haired woman at the checkout desk. I guessed it was Marion Bradley's day off. At first, all I could find were books on how to play electric guitar and tin whistle, but after a couple of questions and a bored finger point from the librarian, I found one book on stringed instruments, and a fingering chart for the cello.

"You learning the cello?" She flashed the scanner's red light over the stickers on the backs of my books. "Cool. I play the concert marimbas."

"Is that a kind of drum?"

"It's like a giant xylophone. You should come out and audition for the orchestra. We're kind of light in the strings section."

"I'm just learning. I can't even read music yet." I tucked

my books under my arm. "Haven't even figured out the bow part yet. So far I sound like a dying moose on the thing."

"Maybe you need to tune it up. It'll tell you how in the blue book you've got. You'll need a tuning fork, or something."

I thanked her and jumped back in my truck. Tune the thing. Why hadn't I thought of that? And since when did Drumheller have an orchestra?

Even taking my time along the back roads, it took less than two hours before the road widened and turned to chip seal and then tarmac and fed me on to the #1, straight into Calgary. I smoked as I drove and listened to my new Johnny Cash CD all the way there. Johnny Cash always reminded me of the smell of the stuff my dad used to put in his hair, and the taste of those little wine-tipped cigars, and Old Spice aftershave. He used to put Johnny Cash on the record player in the front room when he and my mom were heading out on the town for the night. She'd be up in their bedroom, fixing herself up. He would swirl the ice cubes in his drink and tell me stories.

"Never rush a lady out the door while she's doing herself up," he'd tell me. "Shows a lack of foresight."

The Capri Motor Court and Inn had only non-smoking rooms left. I gave the guy my credit card and he wheezed around behind the counter, printing up the papers. A tiny television droned from his desk in the corner, next to a plate of ravioli impaled by a plastic fork.

"Check-out time is eleven a.m." He slid the form across the counter for me to sign. "Your room is around back, overlooking the pool. Which is closed to the public right now, until spring. Ice machine is on the first floor, east side of the building. Off-sales are available from the lounge until

60

eleven p.m., unless she takes a shine to you." He surveyed me, from the boots up. "And she might just take a shine to you. Cigarette machine is in the hall right outside the lobby."

I pulled the bedspread off the bed closest to the heater, folded it, and put it into the closet. I had seen more than enough episodes of *CSI*, when they use that blue light to show where all the bodily fluids were hiding. The place seemed clean enough, though. I liked the smell of the shampoo in the little bottle on the counter. I hauled in the cello and my bag, put them both on the other bed.

I needed some lunch, a newspaper, and a street map of Calgary. Plus, I was running out of smokes. I left the truck in the parking lot around the corner from the row of identical turquoise motel room doors and walked several blocks until I found a little strip of street with a couple of stores and a tiny restaurant. The guy behind the counter had short dirty-brown dreadlocks and a silver ring through his eyebrow. I ordered and grabbed a table in the sunny window, next to a woman wearing a poncho and scribbling in a sketchbook. None of the newspapers were less than a week old.

I borrowed a pencil from the guy with the eyebrow-ring and started with the classified ads. There were classical guitar lessons, piano lessons, drum classes, and three serious players looking for a bassist with strong metal influences. No mention of cellos at all. I folded up the paper and ate my chicken salad sandwich. There were green grape slices in it, and the mayonnaise had curry in it, which at first I thought was weird, but I liked it anyways.

I figured I should get a map and find Allyson's place. Get it over with. The thought of seeing her hung around my neck like a lead scarf. What would a guy say?

I called her from a payphone outside a barber's shop. It picked up right away, went straight to the machine. Both of their voices, speaking in tandem: *Hi there, you've reached Kathleen and Ally's place.* I hit the number key so I didn't have to hear the rest of their message, what they were doing instead of answering their phone, what I could leave after the beep.

"Hi, um, this is Joey. I'm in Calgary for a couple of days, and I've got the last of your stuff in my truck. You can call me at the Capri Motor Court, room 119, and leave a message when you'll be around. I guess that's it."

I hung up hard, wishing I didn't always sound like such a fucking idiot on the voicemail. For some reason, answering machines always made my heart pound. Something about my words being on a machine; a permanent record of me not knowing what to say.

I bought a pack of smokes, a map, a box of crackers, some cheese, and a chunk of summer sausage. A paperback novel, and a new toothbrush. Something about a road trip that called for a new toothbrush. Took them all back to the motel. I pulled back the pumpkin-coloured curtains in my room, and blocked the front door open with the wooden wedge I found next to the wastepaper basket. I sat down on the chilly blue bench that was bolted to the concrete sidewalk outside my front door. I smoked, staring at the scabby patch of grass between where the sidewalk ended and the chain link fence around the swimming pool began. The water had been drained out, the bottom covered with a layer of once orange and red leaves, and a flattened Styrofoam hamburger box.

I missed my dog already.

I took out the map, the yellow sticky note with Ally's address on it, and the cowboy's postcard. If I was reading things right, Ally's place and the cowboy's ex-wife lived at completely opposite ends of the city. I'd have to take the truck with me tomorrow. Today, I was going to just chill, read my book. Maybe take a nap.

The door of the room next to mine opened up and an older man came out, wearing navy blue work pants and a pair of spotless new steel-toed boots. He sat down at the other end of the bench and pulled out a pack of rolling tobacco.

"You want a tailor-made?" I extended my pack.

"Don't mind too much if I do, thank you."

He extended a still muscular arm across the bench and I shook a smoke out of my pack for him. Working-man hands. Gold watch, no rings.

He rattled a box of wooden matches in his left hand, slid it open with his thumb and shook one out. Lit the match by flicking the tip with a wide thumbnail. My mom's brother, my Uncle Reg, used to be able to do that. Now his hands shook too much from the MS.

"Name is Hector McHugh." He dangled the smoke from the corner of one lip and shook my hand.

"Joseph Cooper. Nice to meet you, Mr McHugh."

"Hector, please. No need to mister me."

"Hector."

He stared past the swimming pool, over the tracks, down the hill towards the city. "Not a bad view from this spot, once it gets dark and the lights go on. I've been here for six weeks now."

I lit another smoke. So much for quitting. "Six weeks. You working in town for a while?"

"I'm retired."

"You're living here then?"

"I would call it more like resting. I've found myself at a bit of a crossroads."

I nodded. If he wanted me to know what his choice of roads looked like, he'd tell me.

"I used to work as an expeditor, for an outfit out of Edmonton. Diamonds. Northwest Territories are riddled with them. Mining camps and teams of surveyors and drillers all over the place, and they all need supplies. I was the man who found said supplies and acquired them, and saw to it that they were delivered. I kept a small apartment in Edmonton, but the better part of the time I was on the road. It's a fine job, if you like to see the lesser travelled regions of the country."

I just let him go. I could tell he needed someone to listen to him.

"Had a close call last spring. A little Cessna four-seater. Engine failure, over a particularly desolate stretch of the tundra. I thought that pilot was going to be the last soul I ever set my eyes on. I found myself apologizing to God for all my misdeeds."

Hector raised his wiry eyebrows, to see if I was still listening. "And I'm not much of a religious man."

"What happened?"

"The pilot managed to bring the plane down in a little lake, which scared the shit out of me even more than all those pine trees coming at us so fast. I'm not much of a swimmer, you see. But once I got the wind back into me, I

64

hung on to the cushion from my seat, and a guy in a speed-boat picked me up after about ten minutes. Couldn't move my legs when he dragged me into the boat, though. Water's still pretty icy in May."

"The pilot?"

"Christopher. His name was Christopher Dawson. Young fellow, full of piss. He told me to hang on to something, that he was going to swim to shore and bring back some help." Hector leaned over and dropped the cherry of his cigarette butt onto the concrete. Crushed it methodically with the tip of one boot, then slowly bent over to retrieve it. He dropped the butt into a tin bucket next to the bench and reached into his sweater pocket again for his pouch of tobacco.

"So by the time this guy drags me into his boat and we head off to find Christopher, it was too late. Took three days for them to drag the lake for his body. Coroner said the hypothermia probably got to him almost immediately because he was swimming so fast, and because he was in such good shape."

I raised my eyebrow in a question mark.

"No body fat. No insulation. Swimming exposes the parts of the body that dissipate the most heat into the cold water. Myself, I have a bit of extra around the middle, and I did nothing but float around. That's what saved me. Being a bit overweight and waiting around to be rescued." He ran his tongue along the edge of the cigarette paper, gave it a twist, bit the end off, and spat it out. "Haven't been able to get myself on an airplane since."

The highway below us was turning into a caterpillar of headlights.

"Interest you in a bit of a drink, Joseph? How do you feel about single malt scotch?"

I folded up my map, stuffed it inside my coat, and followed Hector into the light escaping from his open door.

Hector's room was identical to mine, just flipped in reverse. He unwrapped the paper from a clean glass and dropped two ice cubes into it, followed by a healthy shot of scotch. It warmed my throat on its way down and collected in a hot pool in my belly.

Hector had pulled the bedspread off one of the beds in his room too, and replaced it with a heavy checkered blanket. His leather shaving kit was laid out neatly beside the little sink outside of the bathroom, his clothes hung up in the closet. Four identical pairs of work pants, denim shirts in several shades of faded, one brown suit, and one white shirt still in the drycleaner's plastic. The television glowed into the middle of the room, its sound turned right down.

A brand new laptop shined silver and out of place on the bedside table, its charger plugged into the brass outlet in the base of the reading lamp.

"Like my new toy?" Hector ran the palm of one hand over the computer. "It's not even a week old. I'm writing a book." He looked proud of himself.

"A book? What's it about then?"

"Two fellows who work a ranch together."

"A cowboy type thing?"

"Something of the sort." Hector pulled the straight back chair out from the little desk, dragged it on two legs into the centre of the room. "Have a seat, Joseph, and tell me what brings you to the Capri Motor Court. You in town for business?"

"Pleasure, I guess. If pleasure is the opposite of business. I run a garage in Drumheller. I'm just in the city for a couple of days. A holiday, I guess. Couple people I need to see. And I'm looking for a cello teacher."

"You've got kids then?"

I shook my head. Guess I didn't much look the musical type. "It's for me, actually. I'm just learning. Don't really know which end to start with, though, so I need a little help."

"You're the first cello player I ever met."

I looked directly at Hector for the first time. What was left of his silver hair was cropped real short, almost shaved. His moustache and beard were neatly clipped, all straight lines. I put him in his early sixties.

"You're the first writer I ever met." I rattled the ice cubes in my glass.

He took off his sweater and hung it on the edge of the little suitcase rack next to the desk, then leaned over with the bottle of scotch and poured us both another shot. His hands were steady. Not a hard boozer, unless he was one of those guys who you could never tell were always plastered. Franco used to be like that, in his early days.

Hector's T-shirt looked like it had just come out of the plastic wrapping, the fold lines still in it. He took a sip and made a face. "That'll cure what ails you." Fixed his brown eyes on me. "You married, Joseph?"

He had a way of staring right at me when he asked a question that kind of threw me off. Like he asked because he wanted to know, not just to make conversation.

"Divorced. About a year ago."

Hector waited for me to continue, his eyes dark brown

68

and crinkled at the edges. I could feel the scotch working its warm way into my arms and hands.

"Actually, one of the reasons I came to Calgary is because I need to drop off the last of her stuff. She's living here now, with her new … partner."

"She's remarried already?" Hector winced, sympathetic. "She didn't run off on you with one of your buddies, did she?"

"Not exactly." I was about to leave it there, but for some reason it wouldn't stay. "We were married for five years, and I was crazy in love. She changed my life. I thought we were going to you know, do the whole thing. Get old together, teach the grandkids to water-ski. I learned to like vegetarian food. She'd been to Europe."

I stopped, but Hector didn't say anything. Just motioned for me to go on.

"So there I was, thinking I was the luckiest guy I knew, until a year and a half or so ago. Me and Ally had been trying to have a baby for a while and it's not happening, so she has some tests done and then I have some tests done, and it turns out, it's me who's, you know, shooting blanks. So I guess I went through a hard time about it all, and she swore up and down that it didn't matter. But then last October she sits me down at our kitchen table and tells me it's over. She's leaving. And then she does, like, the next day."

I drained my drink. Hector held the bottle out, but I shook my head. My lips were already numb, and it wasn't even six o'clock yet.

"She leaves town with the wife of this guy I play hockey with. They leave together."

I looked at Hector to see if he was following me, but I

couldn't tell. I didn't know why I was telling him all this. I guess it was because of his eyes, and his story about the airplane and the lake. How the young guy died and the old guy didn't. How when he asked me a question, I felt like had to tell him the real answer, because any minute either one of us could be gone.

"Together. As in lovers. The two of them."

Hector sat back in his chair, like he was thinking about what I said, as opposed to thinking about what he was going to say back. So I kept talking.

"They are lesbians. Together."

"I understood the first time around, Joseph. I just didn't want to interrupt you. Go on."

All of a sudden I felt like my chair was too small for my ass, like I had just woke up shirtless in front of someone I didn't know.

"That's it. I'm in town to drop off her books, so I can move on. Get a hobby. I'm learning the cello. It's either that, or my mom and sister'll put me on the Prozac. I've been a little hard to be around, they tell me."

"That's understandable, given your circumstances."

"I don't know why I talked your ear off about my sorry love life like that."

"Because I asked."

"Well, thanks for the drink, Hector. And the chat. It was really nice to meet you."

He got up to shake hands. "The pleasure has been mine. You're much more fun to talk to than the woman next door. Gin. Makes for a bitter outlook. Come by any time, Joseph, I'm here most of the time, typing away. I'm always up for some company, so don't be shy to knock."

The scotch was making me itch for another cigarette, plus I was thirsty. I felt around in my pocket for change and went in search of the drink machine. A small bottle of water cost $1.75. Freaky, when you thought about the fact that the Americans were scrapping on the other side of the world for oil, and here we were whining about paying ninety cents for a litre of gas for the truck, meanwhile they're dinging us twice the price for drinking water, right here next to the Rocky Mountains. That was the kind of thing that would drive Allyson to fire off a stern letter to some CEO somewhere. She was a seasoned veteran of the stern letter. In the five short years she had been in Drumheller, she had headed up the letter writing brigade that had single-handedly forced the city to put speed bumps in the school zones, stopped them from backfilling the marsh off of Highway 26, and shut down the fertilizer factory until the company properly installed filters in its smokestacks.

There was another blue bench, identical to Hector's and mine, bolted to the sidewalk in the little outdoor courtyard where the ice and pop machine stood humming in the dusk. I sat down and lit a cigarette, my bottle of water between my knees, weeping condensation onto my good pants. There were four stone and cement planters, evenly spaced on each corner of the courtyard, empty except for beer caps. Stand-up ashtrays full of white sand and cigarette butts next to both doors.

A little girl about six years old suddenly burst through the door that led to the rooms looking out onto the road. She had a ring of dried tomato sauce around her mouth, and she was dragging a plastic basket full of freshly folded laundry. The smell of warm air and fabric softener hung in the air she brought out with her. A young woman in a matching velour tracksuit and flip-flops followed her, ten feet or so behind.

"Hold the door for Mommy, Raylene, my hands are full."

I jumped to my feet to hold the door open for her. Mommy? She didn't look like she could even be twenty. She must have had the kid when she was still a baby herself.

"Thank the nice man, Bug." She had an overstuffed garbage bag in both arms and was pushing a wicker basket through the door with one flip-flop.

"Thank you." The little girl suddenly went shy, popping one thumb into her mouth and reaching sideways through the air with her other hand for the leg of her mother's track pants.

I nodded you're welcome and picked up the little girl's basket with one hand and the top of the bag of laundry with the other.

"Here, let me help you with that."

The young woman let the bag go into my hand, relieved.

"Thank you so much. We just washed seven loads, didn't we, Bug? My name is Kelly. This is my daughter Raylene."

We shook hands in the air without touching, on account of all the laundry. Raylene sucked her thumb and avoided looking right at me, twisting her upper body in half circles, alternating from side to side. Her hair was exactly the same red-blonde shade as her mother's. Same nose, too.

They were staying in the corner suite, right next to the parking lot off the highway. Kelly had the key for her motel room on a ring with the rest of her keys and an orange rabbit's foot keychain. She held the wicker basket against the stucco wall beside her door with one hip and unlocked the door, kicking it open with her knee.

Their room had a tiny little kitchenette, the remnants of their spaghetti dinner still on two plates. There were crayon drawings stuck to the mini-fridge with magnetic letters, and three different cereal boxes tucked into one corner of the counter, next to a toaster. Kelly and Raylene were living here in this one big room, with the headlights from the highway scrolling like a lighthouse across the wall over their headboards. A scruffy bit of lawn outside the barred window where the tourists let their poodles shit before loading them back into the minivan.

I dumped the bag and basket on the bed, disturbing a pile of stuffed animals that had been arranged on the pillow. Raylene pushed past me to come to their rescue.

"Sorry, kiddo. Didn't mean to bump anyone. I'll get out of your way. Nice to meet you." I stepped towards the door. "Nice to meet you both."

Kelly was scraping the leftover spaghetti into a plastic bag and putting the dishes in the sink. Under the fluorescent tube in the kitchen, she looked older than she did outside. She had pulled her hair behind her ears, revealing a cluster of earrings, maybe eight or so in all.

"You wouldn't mind lending me a cigarette before you leave, would you?"

I took my pack out and shook three smokes out of the tin foil for her.

"Thanks, James."

"It's Joseph."

She followed me outside, placing one cigarette between her lips and unfolding a lawn chair she had stashed behind her door.

"Read your books, Bug. Mommy's having a smoke. No TV, okay, honey?"

Raylene nodded, still in her puffy coat, sitting on her bed with her feet hanging over the edge.

"And no boots on in the house."

"The carpet is sticky by my bed," Raylene said in her small voice.

Kelly pulled the door shut and sat down in her lawn chair. "Don't mind her. She doesn't like it here much. Do you have a light? I left my pack at work, in my locker."

I lit her cigarette, then mine. Stuffed my one hand into my pocket, leaned my ass against the concrete wall between her front door and the parking lot. Couldn't blame her for wishing she lived somewhere else.

"We're not going to be here much longer, I keep telling her. I'm saving up."

I nodded, stared at the red end of my smoke.

"I work at the Bay, downtown. Part-time cashier. Plus at the Esso, three days a week. You?"

"I run a garage in Drumheller. I'm just in town for a couple of days. Little holiday."

"A holiday at the Capri?" She smiled and blew a perfect smoke ring. "Figures. All the nice guys only stay one or two nights. Just the losers move in here."

"How many people live here full-time? I never heard of that before. Forty-nine dollars a night? That must get expensive."

"Is that what that cheap fucker is charging you per night? That guy, I tell you. You should try to talk him down a bit. That's almost what he charges the Americans. I pay the monthly rate. It's way cheaper. Cheaper than that shitty basement suite me and Raylene were in at first, until we came here. Least this place has no mice, and the hot water works. We're on the waiting list for this co-op, a place for single mothers. I'm a single mother. It has a courtyard, and a weight room, and ping-pong and everything. We're getting a puppy. We got another six weeks in this dump and then we move in there, on New Year's Day. Home sweet home."

"Sounds nice."

"You don't talk much, do you, Joseph?"

"That's what they tell me."

"I like that in a man."

"I'm old enough to be your father."

"I didn't mean that."

"Oh."

I didn't know what to say, so I lit two more smokes and passed one to her. She squished her first butt out with her flip-flop.

"Besides, since when has that stopped your average man?"

"We're not all like that."

"I hope the fuck not. I wouldn't know, though. I've got real bad taste in men." She lowered her voice, looking towards the closed curtain, then back at me. "Raylene's daddy is in Toronto, with one of the girls I used to work with. A friend of mine. Ex-friend of mine, I should say."

"Were you two married?"

"Would that make it suck any less if we weren't?"

"Course not."

"Common-law. Same thing. Besides, we have a kid together. That means more than married any day, at least to me it does. Why? You married?"

"I'm divorced."

"How many kids you have?"

"None."

"See? You guys can both go your own way now, no strings. Not like me and Tony. That bastard's gonna be in my life for-fucking-ever. Or at least his mom will. She doesn't think I can take care of Raylene all by myself, but I'm showing her, we're fine, and no thanks at all to her bastard of a son. I'm working two jobs, plus I'm getting my dog-grooming licence at the vocational school one night a week."

"I guess I should be glad Allyson and I never had a baby. We wanted to. I mean, we were trying."

"You had to try to have a kid? I wish. I had an IUD in when I got pregnant with Raylene. Can't take the pill. Makes my ankles swell up like water balloons."

"That can't be good."

"It's not, believe me. Anyways, too bad about you and your wife. You woulda made a great daddy."

"You don't know that. You just met me."

"A girl can tell these things, just by looking. We've got a special antennae for it. I should go in. We borrowed a VCR for a couple of days from a guy at work. *The Little Mermaid.* Thanks for the smokes. See you around."

Kelly folded up her lawn chair and went inside. I wondered, if she really did possess a special asshole antennae, how come she hadn't used it when it mattered.

It was full on night by the time I got back to my own room, and the red light on the phone was flashing in the dark. The room was chilly and smelled like disinfectant. I turned up the electric heater under the window and it made a buzzing sound, like a tiny airplane was in the room with me. I dialed zero for the front desk. It was Lenny himself.

"Messages for 119? Just the one, where did I put it? Here it is. Allyson called you back. She's out for the evening. Wants you to call her in the morning. You got enough clean towels?"

I told him I was just fine, thanks, and hung up the phone.

I was laying on my bed, my coat and boots still on, when someone knocked once on my door. It was Hector.

"Joseph. I'm heading up to the Wong Kee for the all-you-can-eat deal. Would you like to join me? The food is pretty good, and I'm buying."

"Sure, Hector, that'd be good." I hadn't thought of dinner yet, and some company would be nice. Ally couldn't stomach Chinese food. The MSG always made her break out in a rash.

Hector had a suede coat on, the exact same colour as his brand new workboots. He had shaved, too, and smelled like cologne.

We took Hector's truck, a little Datsun about twenty years old, painted that green colour they made them back then. Still in good shape, no rust.

"Diesel costs more these days than gas." Hector turned the key and waited for the glow plug to light up. "Not exactly what I had in mind when I bought it."

"I used to drive a truck just like this when I was a kid. It was my first set of wheels. I loved that little truck. Mine was white." I ran my hand over the gearshift, remembering how Sandra Jennings used to bitch about catching the hem of her skirt on it when we were fumbling out of our clothes, how the streetlight would light up the beads of condensation dripping down the windshield like pearls. It struck me that I hadn't been laid in over a year, and all of a sudden this seemed wrong to me.

Hector saw me eyeing a notepad and pencil taped to a string, stuck right on the dashboard.

"That's for when I think of things I want to write about while I'm driving." He flipped over the top page of the pad, to hide what was written.

"I met another one of our neighbours tonight, after I had that drink with you. The single mom and her little girl."

"Kelly and Raylene. She's quite a remarkable young woman. Let me guess. She borrowed a cigarette from you?"

I nodded.

"That's how I met her, too. I don't think she can afford to smoke, poor girl. Raising the kid up all by herself."

"I'll never understand how a guy could run off like that, and leave his own wife and kid to live in a motel."

"It sounds to me as though she'll be better off without him around anyway. He's a meth head."

"A what?"

"Crystal meth. Nasty drug. Both those kids are better

78

off without that business around. Kelly's got a good head. They'll be fine on their own."

"Maybe, but they shouldn't have to be."

"People make their own beds though, too, Joseph. She obviously made some bad decisions somewhere along the way. Life has consequences. Sooner she figures that out, the better. Who's to know what passes between two people, anyway? What she was like to live with? All we ever hear is one side of the story."

We were parked outside the restaurant now. Hector turned off the ignition, but didn't take his hand off the key, just sat there, waiting for me to respond.

"So don't you think sometimes it's just the one person's fault?" I said at last. "All of a sudden one half of a marriage decides, for whatever reason, that they can't be there anymore, and they just take off, and none of it was the other person's fault? That the person who got left behind just got screwed, like, and they didn't bring it upon themselves somehow?"

Hector pulled his key out of the ignition. "Do I ever think a divorce is the fault of only one half of the equation? I'd have to say hardly ever. Very rarely."

We sat there for another minute, both of us staring straight ahead into our own thoughts.

"Let's go eat, Joseph. Lock your door. You're in the city now."

Hector was right. The food was good and cheap, and we both stuffed our faces without hardly stopping to talk at all. The place wasn't long on ambiance. The waitress had long dirty blonde hair and mostly sat behind the take-out counter in the corner, talking on the phone. Every once in a while she'd set the phone down and make a quick round with the ice water to appease the few tables that had any-body eating at them, and then return to her stool to talk, the phone cord coiled around her fingers.

Hector insisted on picking up the tab, even tipped the phone-talker a fiver, which I didn't think she deserved. She did get off the phone to take our money, I will give her that.

On the way back to the motel, Hector pulled over at a 7-Eleven and came back with two pouches of Number Seven tobacco, one of those little rolling machines, and a box of cigarette tubes.

"Does rolling your own save you much money? Seems like a pain in the ass to me."

"I like to roll my own. I like the ritual. These are for Kelly."

I looked sideways at the old man. "I thought you said she had made her own bed?"

"I did. Didn't say a guy couldn't give her a hand up here and there, though, slip her a few luxury items. It's not like the deadbeat that knocked her up is helping her out."

"How come you're living in a motel, anyway? Can't you find a little apartment for cheaper? More space?"

"What's wrong with the Capri? It's clean enough. I don't need much space. Besides, this way I don't have to wash my own sheets and towels. I'll probably buy a little place when I figure out where I want to live. What I want to be when I grow up."

"You could have a little more privacy in an apartment, is all, I guess. Quieter."

"Who says I want privacy? I like my room. I get out to eat, I meet people. No people friendlier than folks who think they'll never see you again."

"That right?"

"Absolutely. You haven't travelled much, have you?"

"Been to Mexico once, on our honeymoon."

"Oh, you have to travel. Travel alone. That's how you have the greatest adventures. Even all through my marriage, I still travelled alone, for work of course, and then some. Sometimes my wife came with me, but sometimes not. Those were the best trips. Europe. Southeast Asia. You should get off the continent. Do you good."

"You were married? You never mentioned her."

Our headlights rolled over the motel parking lot, scared a big tomcat into the shrubs.

Hector coughed a little. "No, I didn't. That's a whole other story. We'll save it for another night. Sleep well, Joseph."

Hector went straight into his room. A few minutes later, I heard music through the wall. He was listening to Nina Simone. Sounded like, "Oh Sinner Man, Where You Going to Run To?"

The next morning, Kelly was sitting outside on her lawn chair in her Esso uniform, rolling cigarettes with her new machine. A cup of coffee was steaming on the cement ledge next to her.

She waved hello as I jumped into my truck. She was wearing eyeshadow. Looked younger than before, like a teenager.

I rolled the window down. "I'm out for the day. You need anything?"

"You going into town? You could drop me and Raylene off at her daycare, if you're not in a hurry. It's about twelve blocks. I have to be at work at eight. We can be ready in two minutes."

"Take your time, Kelly. I'm not in a rush."

Raylene still looked half asleep under her toque and winter coat when she came out. Her eyes were red, like she'd been crying.

"Joseph's going to give us a ride, so you'll be early for daycare. You'll have time to play on the swings. Say thank you to Joseph," Kelly said as she squeezed in beside me so that Raylene could have the spot with the seatbelt, but Raylene wouldn't speak. Instead, she breathed a circle of fog on the passenger window, then drew a shape of a tree in it with her tiny finger.

"Sorry, Joseph. She's not a morning person. Neither of us are."

"Don't worry. I'm not much of a conversationalist at the best of times."

When I dropped them off, Kelly held up one of Raylene's hands and waved it at me.

"Thank you," she mouthed at me through the windshield. I tapped the horn and pulled back out into traffic. I was going to try the cowboy's ex-wife's place first, in Mount Royal, then I'd try calling Allyson. I'd been thinking maybe Ally could help me find a cello teacher, maybe she could put up an ad for me at the art school she was going to.

I drove around for a while, even had to pull out the map to find Cecelia Carson's house. It was an old, two-storey place, with a closed-in sunroom for a porch. An unruly holly hedge caught at my coat as I walked up to the front door. A "Beware of Dog" sign hung in the window, and a "Please, No Flyers" sign above that. I could hear a small dog barking furiously from inside, but I couldn't bring myself to beware of it.

I knocked and waited for a minute, then knocked again, the dog inside working itself into a fluffy-sounding frenzy on the other side of the door. No one answered, so I turned to leave. On the top step, next to a withered pot of Black-Eyed Susans, was a magazine, rolled up and wrapped in a plastic bag. Too big for the mail-slot in the door. It was a copy of a ceramic arts magazine, and it was addressed to Ms Cecelia Carson.

So maybe Jim Carson's wife was really an ex. She called herself Ms, and was apparently into pottery.

I jumped back into my truck, glancing at my watch, a Christmas gift from Allyson. The stainless-steel band always got caught in the hair on my arms, but I never told her, and wore it everyday anyway. It was only a quarter to nine; too early to go by Ally's yet. I would stop somewhere for breakfast and call her beforehand. Then I'd come back here to try and talk to Ms Carson tonight, after the supper hour was over.

I got stuck trying not to go the wrong way up a one-way street and couldn't find the little joint with the chicken salad from the day before. I ended up parking outside a diner that said it had a $3.99 breakfast special. It smelled like bacon and drip coffee, just like home.

The waitress called me sweetheart, let me take a booth in the window all to myself, and brought me the *Herald* to read. She delivered me my food almost right away, left me a carafe of coffee, and told me she'd be in the back booth having a smoke when I was ready to pay.

"Got to get off the old dogs for a minute before we get the lunch rush in. You're the calm before the storm," she said, one hand massaging her lower back.

I took my time eating, listening to Neil Diamond from the tinny speakers bolted to the wood paneling above my head. I ate everything on my plate, then found the waitress in the back and asked if I could borrow her phone. She heaved herself up from her crossword and dragged the receiver on a long cord across the counter, then dialed the number for me. It went straight to Ally and Kathleen's voice mail, meaning they were home, and on the phone. I hung up without leaving a message.

I paid with a ten, told the waitress to keep the change.

"Well, sweetheart, why don't you come back here tomorrow when the breakfast rush is here, and show that lot what a real tip looks like."

"I'll be sure and do that," I smiled at her. She should be retired by now, I thought, not worrying about resting up her dogs for the lunch rush. That was something I noticed in the last ten years or so, older women working in Tim

Horton's or at the drive-through, stuff you used to only see teenagers doing.

Ally and Kathleen lived in one of those artist's loft type deals in a part of Calgary the map called Kensington. Mostly antique stores, coffee shops. I could see how Ally would like living in a part of the city like this. Kathleen, I realized, I knew next to nothing about, except that she used to teach kindergarten in Drumheller. I started having second thoughts, imagining the three of us sitting around a table, them still in their bathrobes, shiny in their love bubble, and me in my good grey pants. Ally would know I had dressed up for the occasion.

Maybe I should find a phone and try calling again, just meet her somewhere neutral-like. I was standing in front of their intercom, my forefinger dangling in indecision, when I heard a voice from behind and above me.

"Joey? Is that you?" It was Kathleen, from a second-storey window on the other side of the courtyard. "Here, I'll buzz you in."

The hallway had at least fourteen-foot ceilings and was tiled with red and white octagons. There were three or four mountain bikes locked to the oak banister that curled up towards the second and third floors. Six brass mailboxes in a row right inside the door, and a recycling box. I could smell fresh coffee, and the lazy tang of marijuana. A cork message board announced a board meeting and a clothing swap.

Kathleen met me as I reached the top of the stairs. She looked pretty much the same as the last time I saw her, when she was sitting in the driver's seat of Mitch Sawyer's new truck in my driveway. Staring anywhere but at me while Ally loaded her stuff into the canopy. I didn't help her with her bags.

Buck Buck had whined and followed Ally back and forth from the truck to the garage door, thinking maybe we were going camping, then sat down at my feet in the front yard and pressed his body up against my leg. Suddenly, I missed my dog.

"Joseph, you look good. Come on in. Ally just went to get bagels. She'll be back in a minute."

Fuck me, I thought. Ally was never back from anywhere in just a minute. I was going to have to sit and think of things to say to Kathleen. What did we have to talk about? How's my wife, Kathleen? I mean, how is she? All the coffee I drank at breakfast was rolling inside my belly, threatening to make an appearance again. My mouth started to sour with jealousy, something I hadn't much allowed myself to indulge in since this whole thing had gone down. Mostly all I had felt until that moment was plain old sad.

But I followed Kathleen towards their propped-open front door, making small talk about how the roads were and whatever. Then I remembered Ally's boxes in my truck.

"Hey Kathleen, how about I go grab Ally's stuff right now, and bring it up. I'll be right back."

I turned around to leave, but Kathleen put her hand on my arm.

"Actually, Joey, I'd like it if just you and I could have a word alone before she gets back. The stuff can wait. You're not in a rush, are you? Your mom says you're staying until Friday, right?"

I took a deep breath and bent down to untie my boots.

I followed her into their apartment. Hardwood floors,

brick walls, one big open main floor with a half-loft upstairs. An easel in the bay window. A large island counter in the centre of the corner kitchen, with tall oak stools tucked around it. A stainless steel fridge and stove. I seriously thought for a second a vein was going to pop right out of my forehead.

"Can I use your washroom?" I asked.

"Upstairs, the door on your left."

I splashed cold water on my face, then dried off on a towel that smelled like Ally. Felt like I had a giant elastic band wrapped around my chest, squeezing. I kept looking at my watch like it could tell me something other than the time. I stayed in the bathroom, leaned up against the counter, until it started to feel like I was hiding, then padded back down the stairs in my sock feet.

Kathleen was perched on a stool in the kitchen and motioned me to sit down. She had poured two cups of tea, the loose kind that you steep in a silver ball. Peppermint. I wondered if it was the same batch Ally had harvested the year before from our garden. It had disappeared when Ally did, from the cupboard beside the stove. Or maybe they drank all that together already and this stuff came from their own little garden, or maybe they had gone shopping together, to one of the hippie places Ally liked to go to, where you had to scoop the tea or popcorn or whatever out of a big bin yourself and write down the number on a little tag. One of the places my mom refused to buy anything in, claiming it was unsanitary.

"What I wanted mostly to tell you, Joey, was thank you." Kathleen's eyes were trying to find mine, her face wide and open.

"For bringing the boxes? It was nothing, really, I had to

88

come to the city anyways for a couple of errands and...."

"Not for the boxes. For being so cool about all of this. We both really appreciate it."

I didn't say anything, so she continued.

"I mean, Mitch has been such an asshole about all of this, I can't even tell you how hard it's been. Calling here and saying unspeakable things to Ally, charging up my credit card, and screwing around with me seeing the kids. I mean, the kids are Mitch and Sheila's but still, I lived with them on weekends for seven years, and I love them too, and they want to come visit me, but Mitch told Sheila about Ally and me, and now it's all ... weird, because Sheila's family are born-agains, and well, you probably don't want to hear all this shit about your friend and all, but what I'm saying is that I really want to thank you for not pulling any of that. For being so stand up about all of this."

"Mitch is not my buddy, Kathleen. I know he's been a bit of a fuck-wit, I mean, even the shit with the canoe and all was a bit out of order if you ask me, and I'm sorry all that happened to you. Tell you the truth, I never liked the guy. Even if he is a fine defenseman, I always thought he was a bit of an idiot. No offense."

Kathleen smiled. "None taken. I've never had much luck with men."

I sipped my tea. Didn't know what to say to that, because all the obvious things were unspeakable.

"But you're a really nice guy, Joey, and I want to say that I'm sorry for how things happened."

Just then Allyson burst through the door, with bagels and flowers and library books.

"Joey, oh my God, look at you. You're wearing your good pants. How are you?"

She had cut off most of her black hair. I didn't recognize any of the clothes she was wearing. She looked a bit tanned, especially for November. She looked beautiful. When she leaned over her and hugged me, I could smell the outside on her. She felt leaner, maybe even buff.

"Any more tea?" she asked Kathleen.

Suddenly I could feel a tight wad catch somewhere between my tongue and my chest, squeezing the tea I was trying to swallow. I didn't think I could keep sitting like this, with the two of them, being so ... normal.

I felt my nails get sharp and stick into my palms, and that elastic band around my chest again. Then all of a sudden I sort of lost focus on the things in the corners of my eyes, and everything on the counter in front of me seemed overly detailed and really big, but somehow far away.

I heard a tinkling noise, like a spoon being dropped in a sink, and then I remember thinking white knotty pine paneling, new black boots. Feeling something cool up against my cheek. Something warm in my hair. Something wet.

According to what Kathleen and Ally told me later, I was only out for a minute or so, maybe less, but I have no real memory about any of it until I was slumped in their doorway, Kathleen holding a tea towel full of ice cubes against the top of my head, and Ally on her knees in front of me, trying to stuff my feet into my boots. They limped me down the hall and into the elevator.

"Nice wrought iron work in here," I said. They both looked at me, then at each other.

"How you feeling, Joey?" Ally asked. "You passed right out, cracked your head on the counter. We're going to take you to the emergency. Can you breathe okay?" All the blood seemed gone from her face, leaving a sort of green tinge in her olive skin.

"I ... I think I'm fine." Actually, I wasn't sure. My mouth felt so dry I could barely pull my lips apart enough to speak, and there was a dull drumming inside my skull. Copper-pipe smell of my own blood in my nostrils, my own heartbeat whooshing past my eardrums.

But I knew what she was really asking me.

"Just my fucking head. We can take Mitch's ... your truck. Maybe I shouldn't be driving."

Kathleen drove. There was blood on her shirtsleeve. Ally sat on the bench seat between us. I watched the new flatbed and their red brick building get smaller in the side view mirror. Within three minutes, we were in front of the emergency room doors, and Ally jumped out, reaching one hand up to grab mine and help me out of the truck. It was the first time she had touched my hand in over a year, and her fingers felt cold.

A nurse with a plastic pen on a string around her neck ushered me alone into an examination room right away. Ally stayed behind at the admitting desk to fill out the papers.

"Took a bit of a tumble, did we?" The nurse clucked her tongue and pulled a fresh paper sheet onto the examination bed and motioned for me to lie down. "The doctor will be with you in just a minute. Keep the pressure on. Shall I send your wife in when she's finished?"

The doctor showed up in the doorway just in time to prevent me having to answer. I told her I thought I had maybe fainted, wasn't sure, but that I felt pretty normal now except for the gash in my head. No pain in my chest, no tingling in my extremities.

She pried the towel away and swabbed at my hair, and pulled a rolling tray up to the bed.

"A nasty gash you've got here, for sure. I'm going to give you a local anesthetic and seven or eight stitches."

She opened a drawer, taking out a fresh syringe and a bottle. Unrolled a stretch of stainless steel instruments.

"Have you been under a lot of stress lately, Joseph?" The doctor loaded up the needle. "This might sting a little."

I felt a big sting, and grasped at the paper sheet on the bed, trying to stay motionless. "A lot of stress? I guess that's all relative. I'm going through a bit of a divorce."

"I've never heard of a bit of a divorce." She smiled and reached for a half-moon of a needle. "Is that like being a little bit pregnant?"

"I think so." I could feel my scalp being moved, but I couldn't feel her moving it.

"History of high or low blood pressure, high cholesterol, or heart attacks?"

"My dad died of a heart attack four years ago."

She stopped, looked down at my face for a second. "When was your last check-up?"

"Six weeks ago. My mother. She insists. Everything was fine."

"You ever have anything like this happen before to-day?"

I shook my head. She reached for a tiny pair of scissors, and I felt a far-away tug somewhere above my eyes. She then felt my pulse, then checked my blood pressure. When she was done, she pulled a pink pad from the pocket of her coat, and clicked her pen.

"Your pulse and blood pressure seem normal. I don't think this was about your heart, so you can relax about that. Please, hold out your hands in front of you."

I extended my hands like she had hers, palms down, fingers splayed. They were shaking.

"Have you ever heard of a panic attack, Joseph? Because I strongly suspect that is what you may have just had. Did you experience any dizziness or shortness of breath before you fell? Anything you would describe as an out-of-body experience? Fight-or-flight response? Any inability to concentrate? Excessive perspiration?"

I told her about the teapot getting big in front of my eyes, about the elastic band feeling around my chest, only then becoming aware of the damp circles under my arms.

"My mouth is parched and my armpits are leaking."

She nodded, scribbling on her notepad. "I'm going to suggest you make an appointment with a colleague of mine. She's a therapist. Here's her number. In the meantime, I'm going to recommend you avoid all caffeinated beverages, alcohol or other drugs. Here's a prescription for Tylenol 3's. You're not allergic to codeine, are you?"

I shook my head. "A therapist? You mean this is all just in my head? I made myself pass out?"

There was a quiet knock on the door. Allyson peered in.

"I'm Joey's ... wife. How is he?"

"Your husband is going to be just fine. I've given him eight stitches in his head. You'll need to check on him tonight several times, as he's cracked his noggin pretty hard, and we need to take the usual precautions for a head injury. I've explained to him that I suspect he's had a panic attack, and given him a referral." The doctor ripped the top two pages off of her note pad and passed them to Ally.

"Those are for the inevitable headache he's going to have. Keep him off his feet, and make sure he takes the next few days off work, and makes himself an appointment with Dr Witherspoon."

After the doctor left, Ally slumped into the chair beside me.

"Which one of us do you think should call your mother?" She paused. "I think it should definitely be me."

Ally flipped her cell phone open as soon as we were outside the emergency room doors, and called my mother. She had her on the speed dial. I didn't realize they were still that close. I never got around to things like programming anyone's number into the speed dial. Only in the last couple of years I finally figured out how to make the VCR stop flashing 12:00. Not that I found that kind of thing complicated once I got down to it.

Ally got halfway through a calm explanation of the events of the last hour when my mom took over. Ally paused, listening. "He's fine, Ruth, he's standing right here beside me. Do you want me to put him on the phone? A panic attack, the doctor said. Pan-ic. No, it's not a heart thing, she checked all that out. He didn't really pass out, he fell and hit his head. No, he seems fine now. He's got eight stitches. Okay, I love you, too. Here he is."

Ally passed me the phone, silently mouthing the words, "Calm her down."

"Mom?"

"Joseph, honey, do you need me to come to Calgary? I can have Jeffrey or Sarah drive me, I can be there in a couple of hours."

"I don't need you to come, really, I'm fine. I just cracked my head. A few stitches and a couple of painkillers, and I'm good as new."

"Don't you bullshit me, mister, good as new and painkillers my ass. You're going to march yourself into that doctor first thing tomorrow morning and get to the bottom of this. I'm not going to argue with you about it either. I won't make that mistake again. I'm calling Franco right away, to tell him you'll be gone a few more days. They've got medication for these things now too, things that can be done. And if you pull that bullshit macho dumbass number your father taught you, I swear to God...."

You could always tell when she was worried. Concern really brought out the foul language. "Mom, you're breaking up. I'll call you when I get back to my motel room, okay?"

"Motel room? Are you even listening to me? You're staying with Allyson tonight. You're obviously delirious. She can keep an eye on you. I will not have my only son slipping into a coma in a motel room. Put Allyson back on the phone."

"We'll call you when we get back to her place. I'm hanging up now, Mom."

I flipped the phone shut, took a deep breath, touched my sticky, numb scalp.

"Kathleen is bringing the truck around," Ally said. "We'll take you back to our place, put you on the futon in the living room. We can stop on the way home and get your prescription filled, and I'll make you an appointment for tomorrow." She was talking in clipped, efficient bursts. I used to call it her St John's Ambulance voice, after the guy who taught me first aid when I was a Cub Scout. She used it when someone cut their hand really bad, and when Buck had that tangle with the porcupine out at the lake. And when Dad died. We had only been married for a year, but Ally had gracefully swung into action, making calls and spreading calm and coping, the only one in the family who seemed to already believe that we were somehow going to get through it all, as long as we had a plan, we kept putting one word in front of the other, and following them.

"I'm not staying at your place tonight, Allyson. I really appreciate the thought, but I'll be fine at the motel. Maybe you could drive my truck back for me, get Kathleen to follow us there and drive you home? I seriously feel fine right now."

"Joey, I know it's not the most comfortable situation, but I think we can all put that aside for one night, just until we make sure you're okay."

Kathleen pulled up in the truck, ending the conversation. I got in and slumped against the passenger window, liking its coolness against my forehead. Allyson recounted the doctor's findings to Kathleen, who just listened, mercifully silent. It was mid-afternoon by the time we parked in front of their building. The sky was pale blue and too bright white, seemed to bounce off the inside of my eye sockets. My skull thrummed. I needed a smoke. I wanted to lie down.

"Please, Ally, just drive me and my truck back to the motel. I have a friend in the room next door, Hector. He'll check on me. I promise you, I'll be fine."

Allyson raised her eyebrows, made like she was going to speak, then didn't for a second.

"Okay, but I'm calling you every hour on the hour, and if you don't answer I'm coming over. If you slip into a coma, I'll kill you. Your mother will ride my hide into the next world. I will curse your memory forever."

"Look at my pupils, Ally. If you are going to slip into a coma, your pupils go weird. I'll get Hector to drive me to the doctor in the morning. I feel okay, I swear to Christ I do. I just want to lie down. Alone. Please."

"Give me your keys then, tough guy. Kathleen can follow us there."

Ally let us drive all the way in silence. I had always liked how we used to be able to do that, sometimes sit for hours together around the fire when we were camping, or hike for miles without having to speak, just being quiet together, but alone in our own heads.

She looked small in the driver's seat of my truck, hunched right forward, like only the end of her ass was touching the seat, her hands wrapped into fists around the wheel. She had her thinking face on. I couldn't remember if we had ever been in the new flatbed like this, together, but with her driving. I had never looked at her from the passenger seat before.

Of course I was thinking about my dad, probably all of us were, it was too obvious to not trip over it in your head. Anytime I drove past a hospital, or pulled over to let an ambulance pass, it reminded me.

Already four years had gone by. A Saturday afternoon, the beginning of September, lots of long shadows. He and I had taken the little boat out to the south end of Little Bear Lake, to one of our secret grayling spots.

The willows were heavy with brilliant yellow leaves, the branches leaning down and rippling the lake. I flicked my Zippo open, and the flame stood straight up – there was no wind. A couple of seagulls were loitering in the blue above us, eyeing the three silvery fish we already had in the plastic tub, until an eagle swooshed in above them, and they squawked off in a huff.

My belly was full of the roast beef sandwiches and potato salad my mom had packed for us, and my head was buzzing a little from the three or five beers I had drank. I laid my rod against the gunwale and stood up in the front of the skiff to piss, what was left of my last cigarette dangling from the corner of my mouth. My dad rocked the boat from side to side, trying to get me to pee somewhere I didn't mean to.

"Fuck off, Dad, you're gonna make me piss in your boat."

"Isn't my boat anymore, son. I gave it to you, remember?"

"You just gave it to me for a while, when the transom was leaking. I thought you took it back after I welded it."

"I never took it back."

"You did, when you and Mom went to Montana, remember? You came and got it."

"I borrowed it, I didn't take it back."

"Then why do we keep it in your garage, and not mine?"

"I'm still borrowing it."

We used to talk like that all of the time.

He squinted up at the sun. "It's getting late. We should head out of here pretty quick. Me and your mother have to go to the Bowies' place for dinner."

I always wonder how things would be different now, if it had been me who had sat in the back of the boat that day.

My dad reached out and bent the tip of his casting rod over, hooked the lure to one of the eyelets, and stashed it under the gunwale of the boat. He turned and pulled the ripcord on the tiny outboard motor, which stuttered, then sighed. He yanked on it ten or so times in a row, started to curse under his breath. He checked the primer on the tank, ran his hand along the hose, tweaked the choke a little, pulled the cord a couple more times. Still, nothing.

"Fuck me. Now it smells like it's flooded. Did we bring both oars? Did you drain the carbs on this thing recently? It's been cold at night, maybe there's condensation in the lines."

"Why would I drain the carbs on the outboard? You've had it all summer."

"Because it's your boat. You should really take better care of your belongings."

He turned and pulled the cord, three more times, rapid fire.

"That reminds me, Joey. Don't let me forget I need to...."

He stopped in the middle of his next word, his mouth open, like someone had just pounded him on the back. His face filled up with pale. He dropped the ripcord, and it slapped the air around him as it rewound itself inside the motor casing.

"Dad?"

"My ... it's...." Then his mouth kept making the shapes of words but no sound was coming out. One hand gripped the gunwale, the other opening and closing into a fist, grabbing at the fabric of his shirt, his breath coming fast and shallow.

I almost fell over the side of the boat trying to get him around me so I could take his place next to the outboard. Great beads of milky sweat appeared in his hairline and rolled down his face. I propped him up in the bottom of the boat, wrapped my down vest around his shoulders.

I looked up into the one marshmallow cloud, grabbed the cord, and pulled.

The motor caught, chugged a bit. My prayers were answered. I cranked the throttle up slowly until the idle steadied itself, then opened it wide up.

I left the boat on the beach tied to a fallen pine and half-dragged half-walked my dad over and into his truck. I fished the keys out of his pants, and whirled out of the clearing next to the lake in a burst of dirt road dust and gravel. I barely touched the brakes all the way back out to the highway, talking to him non-stop, a steady stream of "everything is going to be okay we're almost there," shifting gears at top speed and returning my right hand to his shoulder, holding him upright.

I stopped at the cutoff, racing into the Esso and screaming at the guy to call 911, have the ambulance meet us on the highway, the little blue Ford Ranger, my dad has had a heart attack.

He had another one about five minutes and eight kilometres later, on the stretcher on the side of the highway on his way into the ambulance. But it was the third one that actually killed him, fifteen or so minutes later, in the emergency room, just before they got the paddles on him. Just before my mother got there. She had been out back, in the garden, picking greens to make a salad to bring to the Bowies' for dinner, and she hadn't heard the phone at first because for some reason Chester, my dad's little Jack Russell, had been barking non-stop for the last forty-five minutes.

We stopped at a strip mall and Ally ran in to the drugstore to get my codeine prescription. Then I showed her where to turn so she could park my truck as close as she could to the door of my motel room. Kathleen pulled up right next to us.

"Classy place, Joey. A pool and everything."

"Home sweet home. Thanks, Ally. For everything. Hey, let's get your stuff out of the back, while you're here, and load it into the other truck."

"Don't worry about my books. I can get them tomorrow, whenever."

"Might as well, is all I'm saying. The truck is right here. They're pretty heavy."

"What are you going to do about dinner? You want us to go pick you something up? Your mother is going to freak when she finds out I left you alone."

"I'll deal with her. I'm fine, I'm telling you. I can feed myself. I barely even have a headache now. I don't know what the fuck happened, but seriously, all I feel right now is tired."

"Your mom is freaking because of your dad, Joey. You need to call her. Call the doctor, too." She took the pink prescription note out of her pocket and stuffed it into mine, next to my cigarettes. "You need to take this seriously, get it dealt with."

"I'm not like him. I go to the fucking doctor, remember? I've had everything tested. I've jerked off into cups and had a camera up my ass. I'll deal with it. You need to get off my case about it. You're not my wife anymore."

My words hung and stung in the space between us.

"I didn't mean that like it sounded."

She took the keys out of the ignition, passed them across the empty seat between us.

"You're right, Joey. Point taken. But call me later, okay? I love you."

I didn't say anything, mostly because I couldn't talk around the lump of hard caught in my throat. I waved good-bye to Kathleen, locked up my truck, and half-hugged Ally goodbye. She had said it aloud. I was right, we weren't married anymore.

I waited until they had pulled the pick-up out onto the main road, until I was sure they couldn't see me anymore. Then I lit a cigarette.

I spent what turned out to be quite a bit of time in front of the mirror with a wet facecloth, trying to clean the dried blood out of my hair. I'd had stitches in my head a couple of times before, and I knew it was going to be a while until I could fully shower and wash my hair, because I couldn't get my stitches wet. I poured myself a scalding hot bath, though, and climbed in, letting the heat soak the stiffness that was growing in my shoulders and neck. The water swirled pink around my head as I scrubbed my neck and behind my ears. My good white shirt was ruined. It was hanging, rinsed, wrung out, and wrinkled on the single hook on the bathroom door.

Panic attacks? What the fuck was that about? Right in front of Kathleen like that, too. She probably thought I was an idiot. She didn't really know me that much, before. Didn't have much to go on. Not that I should really care too much about how my ex-wife's girlfriend felt about me, but I couldn't help but want her to like me. Truth was, I wanted to like her right back. I think it was because it would have made me feel even worse, if that were possible, if it turned out Ally had left me for someone I thought was an asshole. Truth was, I wanted Kathleen to turn out to be an amazing person, someone Ally couldn't help herself from loving enough to have to leave me. Somehow, I thought, that would take the edge off.

I put on some clean clothes and flopped on the bed in front of the TV. It was five o'clock. I needed to call my mother. I got up, went outside, and knocked on Hector's door. He was wearing a different bright white T-shirt, but the same grey work pants.

"Hector, I need you to do me a favour. Wait two minutes, then knock on my door, really loud. It's really important. I'll explain it later."

Hector shrugged and nodded, started to put his boots on.

I went back to my room and called my mother.

"Thank God, Joseph. I just got off the phone with Ally. You didn't tell me the name of the place you're staying, and it's been almost two hours since the girls dropped you off. I've been just sick with worry. You can't sleep alone tonight. You're not thinking straight."

"I'm not alone, Mom. The guy next door is going to check on me. I'm fine. I've had worse from hockey. I'm going to the other doctor tomorrow, I'm all over it."

Hector rapped on the door, right on cue.

"I gotta go, Mom, my buddy is here. I'll call you tomorrow." I hung up before she could get started.

I let Hector in, pulled the chair out for him.

"That was my mother on the phone. Thank you. What a fucking day I've had. Beer?"

He nodded. I grabbed him one from the little fridge, got myself some water.

"You're not joining me?" He laid his beer cap on the TV table, spun it in a slow circle.

"I'm on the codeine. I fell and cracked my head open today at my ex-wife's new place. I just got back from emergency. Eight stitches." I leaned over and pointed at my head.

"Youch. Should I slip next door and get the scotch?"

"Go ahead, if you want, I shouldn't. Painkillers. I don't take pills very much. I told my mother you were coming over to make sure I don't slip into a coma and drown in the bath or something. She thinks I should be staying at my ex-wife's place tonight. With her new girlfriend."

Hector shook his head, sympathetic. "That would never do."

"Exactly."

"How'd you do yourself in like that? You trip?"

"I wish. It was way weirder than that. I kind of … fainted, I guess. The doctor thinks I had a panic attack. I don't know. I'm supposed to go get checked out fully tomorrow. It's never happened before, so who knows. I didn't think I was that stressed out. But my dad died from a heart attack four years ago, and I guess everybody is freaking out."

"As they should, probably. Stress can do terrible things to a body, let me tell you." Hector tapped his temple with a square-nailed fingertip. "Power of the mind. I had to learn that one the hard way, unfortunately. I lost a bunch of hair, all at once, years ago, when my wife died. Got an ulcer, too. You've got to watch the stress, Joseph."

"Maybe I will have a little belt after all, Hector."

He went next door and came back with the scotch, a heating pad, and a frozen gel icepack wrapped in a clean towel. He poured me just a sliver, left the bottle on the table. Passed me the towel and ice pack.

"Put the ice on your head. Ten minutes on, ten minutes off."

"What's the heating pad for?"

"Your feet. It feels good."

"You're not having a drink?"

"You probably need to just rest for a bit. I'll come by later with some dinner. I'm in the middle of a chapter anyway. Can't stop now. I'll be back in two hours."

I held the towel and ice pack up against my scalp, which felt crispy and hot. Turned the TV on with the remote. I watched about three and a half minutes of the news anchorman talking about an assault on Falujah, then crashed out, on top of the covers.

I woke up in the dark, sweating and heavy headed because I had cranked up the baseboard heater before getting into the tub and forgotten to turn it down. Hector was tapping at the door. I opened it, fanning it back and forth to let some cold air in.

"I don't know if saunas are recommended for those with a head injury," he said, offering me up a steaming plastic bag of take-out. "I hope you like lasagna."

"Lasagna is great." I held open the handles and looked inside. He had brought me a fork, and napkins, and little salt and pepper packets, too. "Thank you, Hector. Let me give you some cash to cover this."

He waved his hand. "I won't hear of it. How does the head feel?"

"I feel okay. Not even much of a headache."

Hector was still standing in the doorway, smelling like aftershave. He had changed his shirt.

"Come on in, I'm sorry. Have you eaten?"

"I'm actually going out to meet a friend. I'll call you later, though, and make sure you don't need anything."

I watched him through my fogged-up window, twirling his key ring around and catching it in his palm as he crossed the parking lot and climbed into his truck. Watched his tail lights turn onto the ramp that led to the highway. He looked kind of spiffed up. Like maybe the old guy had himself a date.

The phone rang. It was Ally. I gave her the same line as

I gave Hector, and promised I'd call her in the morning.

I sat down on the straight back chair. My eyes caught the edge of the cello case in the mirror behind the TV. It had been leaned up against the closet door for two days, untouched. I took it out, pulled the stringed instrument manual out of my bag. The lowest string sounded odd when I plunked it, and I fiddled with the peg that tightened and untightened the string, experimenting with how it changed the sound. Dug around in my brain for what little I had absorbed about music in band class in grades nine and ten. Mostly I had just fucked around with Jimmy Baker, the other trumpet player, and Owen Price on trombone, emptying our spit valves on the girls who were trying to play the flute on the riser below us.

You can only play one note at a time on the trumpet, but you could play up to four at one time on the cello. I knew I had to tune the strings, but I needed something to tune them to. The manual suggested a piano, or a tuning fork, or a pitch pipe. I dug around in the bureau drawer for the phone book to look up music stores. So far I hadn't accomplished any of the things I had come to Calgary for: no cello teacher, no cowboy's wife. I was even still driving around with Ally's stuff in the box of my truck. That wasn't like me.

Again there was a knock on the door. It was Kelly, in jeans and white boots, a baby blue jean jacket. She was holding a clear glass bowl full of green Jell-o cut into squares, with a dab of half-melted whipped cream on top.

"Hey, you. Hector told me you bashed your own head in. I brought you some dessert, leftover from me and Raylene's dinner. Hey, I didn't know you could play anything."

She pushed past me into the room, bringing with her

a cloud of hairspray. She whipped the Saran Wrap off the bowl and pulled a teaspoon out of her back pocket. "Eat up. I need the bowl back for cereal tomorrow."

Of course I couldn't tell her I hated anything flavoured green: Life Savers, Kool-Aid, key lime pie. Always had. I sat down and dutifully spooned Jell-o cubes into my mouth, even though I hadn't even touched the lasagna yet.

She watched me eat every last bit, then took the bowl and rinsed it in the sink. Put it on the bureau by the door, with the spoon in it. Then she leaned toward me.

"So let me see the wound."

I bent down and let her have a look.

"Gross. It doesn't even look real. Looks like a makeup job. Weird. Wanna play me something?"

"I really just got the thing. Just learning. All I can play is the first ten notes or so, from 'I Found My Thrill on Blueberry Hill.'"

"My grandpa used to totally love that song."

Maybe she wasn't even twenty yet.

"How old are you, Kelly?"

"Does it matter?"

"No. Just making conversation."

"Twenty-one. You?"

"Just turned forty in June."

"You look a lot younger. You still have all your hair and stuff."

"Why, thank you."

"Don't mention it. Anyways, I just thought I'd bring you over some dessert, and also, I kind of have a favour to ask you. You totally don't have to say yes or anything, but I just thought I'd ask if you would mind watching Raylene for me tomorrow night. I have my dog grooming class on Fridays, and my friend from work who usually takes her has to go to Canmore because her dad got a hernia operation and can't cook or anything. It's only for three hours, and Raylene'll probably sleep most of the time. She's hardly any trouble at all, especially if she doesn't know you. It would be a really big favour. I'll cook you dinner on Sunday cuz that's my day off, if you're still gonna be here."

"I'll be happy to watch her for a bit, if that's okay by her."

"She'll be fine, I promise. It's my teacher who's giving us the puppy, so Raylene is cool with me going to school. She's into it. I told her she could come to work with me one day, when I'm working with all the animals. She loves animals. Tony was allergic to everything. Only ever let her have goldfish."

"What time is your class?"

"Seven-thirty. Thanks so much, Joey. I knew you were a nice guy. Remember, I said I could always tell. I'd ask Hector, but Raylene says his eyebrows are creepy. Kids are harsh sometimes. She doesn't know too many older men, and I think Hector reminds her of Tony's dad. He was a drunk, and used to take out his false teeth and chase her around with them. Thought it was funny. Then he had a stroke and drooled when he talked. Freaked her out, I think. "

"Bring her by. I'll make sure I'm home by around seven then?"

"Can it be closer to six-thirty? I have to take the bus to my class."

"I'll be here."

"You rock. Do you like pork chops with mushroom sauce? It's me and Raylene's favourite. I always make it on Sundays."

"I love pork chops."

"Cool. I'll let you get back to your music then."

"I was just going to put it away. It's getting kind of late."

"Nobody can hear you on this side, except maybe the old gin lady, and she's probably passed right out by now. Hector's not home. He had a big date." She winked.

"I thought he looked dressed up. I'll have to get the scoop from him tomorrow."

Kelly looked at me. "I doubt he'd tell you much about that."

"Why not? He's a pretty talkative type. He's a writer, they like to tell stories, don't they?"

"Just about other people. That's why he always asks so many questions. He's going to put everyone in his book. He even told me so once. Anyhoo, I should get back. I'll talk to you tomorrow? Thanks again, Joey."

"Thanks for the Jell-o."

She picked up the bowl and pulled the door shut behind her, clicking it softly. She left a waft of hairspray lingering, and something cinnamon, smelled like gum, or maybe it was lip gloss.

I fooled around on the cello some more after Kelly left, liking the way the strings whistled under the callouses that were beginning to bud on the tips of my fingers. I had the TV on real low in the background, one of those Bollywood-type movies was on, where the rich young bachelor wants to marry the beautiful maiden from a lower caste, but her father threatens to kill her if she marries him, and castrate him and all of his brothers and nephews, meanwhile every ten minutes or so everybody breaks out in a killer musical number. I sat with my butt cheeks right on the edge of the mattress and just scronked along with the music.

I still didn't really know how to properly tune the thing, and I have no idea how it must have sounded from the other side of the wall, in Hector's empty room next door, but I had a good time. I learned to cradle the cello with the inside of one leg, giving myself something to lean into as I drew the bow across the strings. I liked how it felt in my body when I managed to get a string to sound, resonant and clear. I could feel it humming in my tailbone, straight up through my back and arms. At eleven o'clock on the nose, I wiped the cello down with the soft rag, carefully laid her inside her case, and stowed her back in the closet.

I knew I should have felt tired after the day I had, but I couldn't even make myself lay down yet. Every time I stopped moving, my brain started turning so fast it made the stitches in my head itch. I put a sweater and coat on, patted my pockets for my lighter and smokes, and headed out for a little walk.

Hector's truck was back already, the cab dark behind the fogged-up windshield. I guessed his date hadn't gone too well.

I found a little footpath on the other side of the ditch alongside the entrance ramp onto the highway, right next to the tree line. It felt good to stretch my legs, and the chill wind stung my nostrils and cooled the burn gathering in the hair follicles surrounding the gash in my scalp.

The path led me alongside the highway for a while, and then through a scruffy field tufted with Safeway bags caught in bare willow branches, broken beer bottles, and an upturned shopping cart missing two wheels. I could smell wood smoke, and underneath that, the tang of car exhaust. The far end of the field sloped down towards the Bow River, and I walked along through the frosted bull rushes and horsetails under an arching steel bridge painted red.

"Buddy, you wouldn't spare a cigarette, would you?"

The voice jolted me out of my thoughts, and I nearly jumped when I first heard it. It belonged to a small man whose face was almost buried in his beard, which was shot through with silvery whiskers stained bronze with nicotine.

This town was hard on a full pack of cigarettes. I opened my pack, pulled back the tin foil from the second half. Shook out two smokes into my other hand.

"Thanks, man." He stood up from the spot of dry gravel he had been sitting on, way up under the eaves of the bridge. It was quieter under here than I would have thought, the cars wheels clicked and thrummed over our heads, but they sounded much further away than they actually were. He had a small fire burning, and there was a ratty grey wool blanket at his feet. When he reached his hand out to re-

trieve the smokes from mine, I could see there had been letters once, a word, tattooed on the backs of the first knuckle
of each finger, but the ink had spread and blurred into fat
blue stick figures.

"Like a swig of wine?"

I shook my head.

He shrugged, flipping one cigarette up between his
teeth and stashing the other in his pocket. "Suit yourself."
He pulled out an ancient silver lighter and lit his cigarette,
then leaned over to block the wind and light mine.

"Cold night," I said.

"Cold, but dry. You can stay warm if you can stay dry."

I nodded, since this was true.

"You looking for a little action then?"

"Beg your pardon?"

"Looking to hook up? There was a fella came through
earlier, I see him around down here couple nights a week,
wears a red down jacket."

"I'm not sure what you mean. I'm not looking for drugs,
if that's what you're asking."

The guy laughed, which set off a volley of deep coughs,
all the way up from his chest. "Buddy, you're in the wrong
part of town if drugs are what you're after."

"I'm just out for a walk."

"Sure, out for a walk. Whatever you want to call it. I
don't care. I was just making conversation, my friend, I
don't care what you do with your spare time. Each to their
own, is what I say."

He shrugged and returned to his little campfire, arrang-
ing the blanket around himself before he sat down again.

I turned and headed back the way I came. It wasn't until I was halfway back across the field, the neon sign in the

Capri's parking lot glowing on my horizon, that it dawned on me what the old guy was talking about.

I thought about guys, strangers, meeting each other under some bridge, out in the cold and the open, and I tried to line it up in my head with Ally and Kathleen, their artist's loft and their stainless steel appliances.

Maybe it was that men were just men, no matter what side of the slice of bread they buttered, and that things were different all around for women when it came right down to the sex thing, gay or not.

Not like I would really know, though, since the only lesbian I knew very well was my ex-wife. There was that postie from Regina that we had for a while at the shop, but it's not like we ever asked her about it or even knew for sure, it was mostly speculation on Franco's part. Said it was about her footwear, and that you could usually tell if you knew what you were looking for, but then Franco says a lot of things.

I told Franco once that I only listened to him about half the time he was yammering on because only twenty percent of what he said was anywhere close to the truth. He thought a bit before answering me, his eyes twinkling, and said that even if only twenty percent of what he said was indeed true, and he maintained his percentage was a lot higher than that, but even at my estimated twenty percent, he was still right more than I was, because I hardly ever fucking said anything at all.

It was a little past midnight by the time I got back to the motel, and the temperature had dropped below zero, I could tell because the parking lot was shiny with frozen dew. I sat down on the little turquoise bench and lit my last smoke of the night. I felt like I could sleep now, after the fresh air.

The cold air made the smoke from my cigarette taste more bitter than usual in the back of my throat, making me feel like puking. As I leaned over and stubbed my smoke out on the frosty cement, the door to Hector's room opened just a few inches.

I saw a cowboy boot first, then a long-bodied guy wearing jeans and a baseball cap slid out, closing the door behind him. He turned quickly, not seeing me sitting right behind him on the bench, and we almost ran into each other right in front of my door. He sucked in a breath and stood back, like I'd scared him.

"Sorry, dude, didn't see you." He quickly nodded, then hustled across the parking lot. A cab pulled up just as he got to the little bedding area full of bark mulch and bare shrubs next to the road. He leaped over the mulch, then the ditch, and opened the cab door. The interior light lit up his face for a minute, clean-shaven, with a thumb-push of a dimple in his chin. He slammed the door shut, then the cab's tail lights disappeared into the dark of the highway on-ramp.

I went inside my room, threw my coat and sweater over the back of the chair, folded my pants and shirt over the arm, and crawled under the covers. I don't remember if I had time to think one single thought before sleep took over.

The next morning the ache in my head was gone, and the only thing my stitches did was itch. My hair felt unwashed already, so to make up for it I had another really hot bath, and shaved meticulously while I soaked. I didn't get out until the skin on the bottoms of my toes began to pucker.

I sat for a while in the chair in my underwear, the phone

on my lap, the pink note from the emergency room doctor in my hand.

Panic attacks. A phone number for a shrink. A motel room to keep my cello in. I didn't recognize my own life. How could this be a day in the life of me?

I called my mom promptly on the stroke of ten, because it was a Friday, and I knew she'd be downtown at Cutters Hair Salon, in the chair closest to the window, getting her hair done by Louise Strickland. Louise didn't have a female customer under the age of sixty, or a male one over the age of ten. She was a grandma and grandson specialist. She did flattops and brush cuts and permanents and sets, that was her established and firm repertoire. Louise was what my mom and the bingo set called a spinster, never had any children of her own. It was rumoured that she bore a life-long disdain for little girls, having been the oldest of five sisters, and the only one to have never wed. My mom and pretty much all the old guard Drumheller gals had always got their hair done by Louise, for the last twenty years or so, anyways, after Louise's dad passed and she found out there was three mortgages on the house they lived in together, all her sisters having married and moved out, and Louise had to go to Edmonton to hairdressing school to keep the roof over her head, and not lose the house her family had lived in since they first found coal in Alberta.

"You have reached the home of Ruth Cooper. Please do leave me a message and I will return your call as soon as possible. Have a lovely day."

"Hi, Mom. Just calling to let you know I feel fine today, my head is fine, but I'm still going to the doctor, just to get everything checked out. Say hi to Buck Buck for me."
I replaced the receiver back on its cradle, balancing it on

my knees. My mom still had an old answering machine, no voice mail. I could see Buck Buck circling and whining in the house, confused because he could hear my voice echoing in the empty kitchen.

I took a huge breath, picked up the phone again, and called the doctor.

"Dr Witherspoon's office." The voice was male, which for some reason I hadn't been expecting.

"Hello, my name is Joseph Cooper, and I was referred to Dr Witherspoon by another doctor at Rockyview General. I'd like to make an appointment to see the doctor today or tomorrow, if that's possible."

"Sir, most of Dr Witherspoon's patients wait for up to a month before seeing her. I can't possibly get you in today or tomorrow." He sounded like I should already know all this. "I can take your name and call you back to let you know how long of a wait you can expect." The guy's tone of voice made me feel like I was being scolded. I didn't like him already.

"Listen, I'm from Drumheller, I'm only in town for a few days. Yesterday I had what the doctor thought was a panic attack. I passed out and cracked my head open. There are no doctors in Drumheller that can handle this type of thing."

I actually had no idea if there were any shrinks in Drumheller, since I never needed one before. But I knew one thing for sure: even if there was someone in town trained for shit like this, I certainly wasn't going to spill my guts to them. All I needed was for Mitch Sawyer or any of those fucking guys to hear about it. This whole deal was best filed away in the same place as my low sperm count, in a cupboard marked my own fucking business.

"Let me speak to the doctor at lunch. Perhaps we can squeeze you in right after her last client. Can you call back around one-thirty?"

"Thanks. I really appreciate it."

I hung up and spent several minutes just sitting there, still in my underwear, staring at my open suitcase on the other bed. What did a guy wear to go see a shrink, anyway? I didn't know anyone who'd ever gone to one. The closest thing I could think of was when Sarah and Jean-Paul went to see a marriage counsellor a few years back, right after Sarah found out about Jean-Paul and the woman who owned the jewellery store, the same place they had bought their wedding rings from eight years ago. Sarah was a mess for a couple of months, all puffy-eyed and volatile, but finally decided not to leave him. They both quit going to the marriage counsellor, and I never asked her why, much less what she had worn when she went.

I finally settled on my default attire: GWG jeans, a white undershirt, and a blue work shirt. The same thing I had worn for the vast majority of my life. I figured dressing up for a shrink might work against me. She might think I'm someone that I'm usually not, and that might take her longer to figure out how to cure me, which would only end up costing me more money.

Panic attacks. I shook my head at myself, trying not to wonder if my dad was somewhere, watching me stumbling through my life, and shaking his head right back at me.

My dad hardly ever came down with a cold, or even a cavity, until that day in the boat. It was flawless, the way he went. Not that it was the way any of us left behind wanted it, but my father died perfectly, keeping in character with the way he had lived. No fuss, no muss. No trouble to anyone, at least not for long. Just the way he probably wanted it. That's what everyone said, anyway, no suffering, it happened so quick, downright efficient even, just like him. I listened and nodded, and never told anyone the truth about the things he had said to me in between breaths that day in his truck. Regrets, mostly, things he wished he would have gotten around to. Where he kept the key to his secret safety deposit box, the one that he had kept all on his own since before he even married my mom. How he had broke down and cried after the second attack, and confessed to me to never tell my mother, but that he had never really believed in a god, undiluted fear making his voice quiver when it passed over his too-white lips. How he always loved me just a little bit more than he ever could Sarah, how he always felt bad about it, and never spoke of it to my mother, but how she always knew anyway.

The hours following my father's death were blurry and out of order in my head, even when they were happening. Allyson had showed up minutes after my mother, who was so inconsolable that one doctor had pulled me aside and suggested that we give her a shot of something to calm her down. Allyson sprang into fierce and focused action. She had planted both of her feet on the weary tiles of the cardiac ward hallway and refused to do any such thing. She had brought a fleece blanket with her from the trunk of her car, which she wrapped around my mother's heaving shoulders, and together we escorted her out of the hospital and into Ally's car, leaning together like teepee poles, holding my mom upright.

At home, my mom refused to lay down, shook her head at the mention of anything to eat, and barely sipped the tea Ally made her. We sat in a stunned circle around the kitchen table. Sarah poured us all a belt of scotch, and Jean-Paul attempted a clumsy toast. My mom's hands shook visibly when she tried to lift her glass, which she touched to her lips without drinking, then put back down on the table. She had stopped sobbing out loud, but tears streamed out of her eyes unabated, tracing the wrinkles in her cheeks on the way down her face.

"Did he say much to you, Joseph? The last thing he said to me on the way out the door was not to put too many snap peas in the salad, that they gave him gas. Then he asked me to keep an eye on Chester."

You couldn't take my dad's dog Chester fishing if you were going to spin cast. He always mistook the spinner leaving the tip of your rod for a stone or a toy you had thrown for him to fetch, and would immediately jump overboard to go get it. After several rescues and fishhook/dog-related incidents, Dad gave up on Chester changing his ways, and only took him trolling. We even tried tying him up to something in the boat, but he would just bark and whine, until you felt like throwing him overboard yourself, just to bring an end to the din.

Buck Buck hated boats, especially little ones.

"Joseph, I asked you a question, honey, are you listening to me? What were your father's last words, please, try to remember them for us. I don't want them to be about that goddamned dog."

Chester's ears perked up. My mom called him that goddamned dog so much, he thought it was his surname.

I opened my mouth and lied to my own mother. Told her nothing I thought she wouldn't want to hear. Told them all how he had talked of how much he loved everyone; how he had had a good life, and was expecting to meet his brother

122

up in heaven. Scrambling for the right words in my mind, the most painless thing to say, something for us all to hold on to.

I had said all the things my father hadn't. At the time, it seemed like the only thing I could bear to do.

Chester stopped eating a day or two after Dad passed away, and crawled under the hedge in the backyard to die not even two weeks later. The vet told us afterwards that Chester's whole insides had been riddled with tumours, probably for months, and claimed it was just a coincidence that he died so soon after my dad, but none of us bought it. Jean-Paul and I snuck into the graveyard in the dark and buried Chester in the frozen dirt at the foot of Dad's grave. The grass seed the landscapers had scattered shortly after the funeral had barely had time to grow roots. The guy who came up with the law against burying pets in the same ground as their humans obviously never had a dog like Chester.

My mom claimed she was too old to even think about getting another puppy.

A wide slice of sunlight burst through the space between the closed curtains and caught the dust that danced when I threw open my suitcase on the bed. The day was in full swing, and here I was sitting around daydreaming. I took out a clean white handkerchief, folded it into a neat square, and tucked it into the inside pocket of my coat, just like my dad had taught me. By the time I got my boots on and left my room, Hector's pick-up was already gone from its usual spot.

I headed in the direction of what I was pretty sure was downtown. I always found Calgary a confusing place to get around in, too may highways that all looked the same, crossing and intersecting at strange angles that everyone from Calgary always swore was a simple grid. I was looking for a music store on 17th Avenue, which I finally managed to find. The place smelled like a cross between a library and a brand new car. It was huge, two floors of grand pianos and racks of acoustic guitars. A long-haired guy wearing headphones was wailing away in a glass booth on what looked like little rubber drums, unheard by the other shoppers. A kid who looked to be barely out of high school approached me, wearing a black dress shirt and a red tie. His gold tag said Rupert, Sales Associate.

"Can I help you find anything?" he asked, sounding uncertain that he could, like maybe I had stumbled in there by accident, looking for a hardware store or something.

"I'm looking for a tuning fork. For a cello."

"They don't make tuning forks for specific instruments. They just make tuning forks. They're over here. You'll probably need an A, I think, but I can check for you. I'm a drum specialist."

He led me over to a glass case and took out a slender metal thing that looked a bit like a divining rod that he placed onto the counter in front of me.

"Anything else I can help you with?"

"Well, maybe. I'm looking for a cello teacher. Don't suppose you'd know of anyone, or somewhere I could go to look?"

"I share a rehearsal space, with, like, five other bands. There's a girl who plays cello in one of them. It's kind of a folk/punk ensemble, her band, but I'm pretty sure she's classically trained and all. I'll call my bass player and get her number. He dated her a couple of times. She's a total hottie."

"That would be great," I said, thinking to myself that Franco was right again. I wondered if I would be able to concentrate with a beautiful young woman teaching me the cello.

"You want to play classical stuff, or more contemporary?" he asked, already cradling the phone with his shoulder, dialing with one finger. He was wearing copper nail polish, I noticed. For some reason I could see the piano guy wearing nail polish, or maybe the singer, but not the drummer.

The bass player picked up right away, saving me from having to answer his question. I had no clue at all what kind of cello I wanted to play. I didn't even know how to tune the thing yet.

"Deano, it's me. There's a guy here looking for a cello teacher, and I thought maybe you knew how to get hold of that girl who plays with the Sally Annes that you dated, what's her name? Yeah, Caroline." He scribbled down a phone number on the back of a flyer. "Catch you later, dude." He hung up and leaned on the counter.

"Here you go, give her a call. She'll probably be able to help you out. Good luck with that. What happened to your head, man? Looks pretty epic."

"Long story." I paid for the tuning fork and stuffed it and the phone number into my coat pocket. "Thanks for everything. I appreciate it."

Outside, a Chinook-type wind had picked up and swirled the leaves around on the sidewalk. I couldn't see a pay phone anywhere nearby, so I pushed my hands into my pockets and took a stroll up the block, away from where my truck was parked. I had shit to do, and the day was wasting.

I ate lunch at a little elbow-shaped café that had a painted cow sculpture bolted to the sidewalk in front of it. Downtown Calgary seemed to contain more creatively painted cows than it did working pay phones. I had a mushroom omelette and something called vegetarian bacon, which turned out to taste kind of like what I imagined oily cardboard would. I flipped through the newspaper, said no to a cup of coffee twice, paid my bill, and then asked to borrow the phone.

I left a message at a place that claimed to be the home of Caroline, Laurie, and Amelia, leaving my plea for a cello teacher and my number at the Capri. I then called Ally to see if she was home so I could finally drop off her stuff, but hung up when the voice mail came on. Then I called the shrink's manservant back. He said I had a stroke of luck, that the doctor's last patient had cancelled, and could I make it in for three-thirty?

I told him I'd be there, and walked back to my truck. It was only one-thirty. I sat in the cab of the flatbed and smoked two cigarettes in a row, unsure what I would do to kill the time. It was probably too early to go by Cecilia Carson's again, and there was no one home at Allyson and Kathleen's. I felt a bit adrift without a task.

I spent over an hour in a used record store that smelled of dust and the incense they burned to hide the yeasty smell coming from the sub shop next door, and ended up buying *Abbey Road* and *Tea for the Tillerman*. But I still arrived at the shrink's almost half an hour early.

The magazines in the waiting room were mostly for ladies, with the exception of an old issue of *Time* and a coverless *Maclean's*. I occupied myself by counting how many times I could find the word "America" in the Canadian magazine, and vice versa, until the receptionist called my name. I looked up in time to see the previous patient walk past me and head for the elevator, looking like a bad photocopy of herself. I wondered if she had looked any better on her way in.

I walked down the hall and through the open office door. I sat down on a stuffed chair and waited, trying to make like this was no big deal, like I did this kind of thing all the time.

The doctor entered, the sound of her heels swallowed by the carpet on the floor. She was what my mom would call a handsome woman, in her mid-fifties. Straight black hair, run all through with grey. No makeup, at least that I could see. No wedding ring. She wasn't a big woman, but she took up a lot of space behind her rosewood desk. A tight, neutral smile on her thin lips.

"So, Joseph. Why don't you tell me what you're here for?"

"Well, yesterday I guess I had a little … episode. I kind of, sort of, fainted, and the doctor at the emergency room said I might have had a panic attack. I don't know. I cracked my head open. It gave everyone a bit of a scare, because my dad died four years ago from a heart attack. Sudden, like. So, I'm here to get it all checked out. My stress levels, that kind of thing."

"Has this ever happened before? Any memory of other incidents, maybe something similar, but less severe?"

I thought for a minute, then shook my head, my fingers

finding the seam along one side of my jeans and tracing it. "Not that I can recall. I don't really even think of myself as a high-strung kind of guy, I mean, I run a little garage, it's not like I'm a stockbroker or a brain surgeon, some kind of a life-or-death type of occupation. Normally I'm pretty well … normal."

Fuck, I thought, at least try to make sense. She's going to think you've got brain damage.

"And how do you feel about what happened to you yesterday?"

"Embarrassed, mostly, I guess. I bled all over my wife's … girlfriend. And now my mom is worried and driving me nuts."

"You feel embarrassed because the attack happened in front of somebody else, and you're only here to reassure your mother? Is there any part of yourself that is here for you, for yourself?"

"Well, yeah. That too. Of course."

She wrote something down on her notepad. I wondered if they let you read all that stuff later. Would the guy working the front desk photocopy everything when things were slow and send it to Drumheller, where someone else would file it, along with the results of my sperm count tests and prostate exam? X-rays of the time I broke my wrist? I looked around for a little tape recorder or camera. Didn't want to ask, in case it made me look paranoid.

"Joseph, I'd like you to describe for me the events of the last few days leading up to what happened yesterday. I'm especially interested in the events of the morning just prior to your attack. What was on your mind. If there was anything unusual or difficult happening, that kind of thing."

I started off with the Allyson stuff, because that seemed

the most obvious. I meant to just tell her the basics, the who and what and where, but I ended up stammering on and blabbing about everything, all of it, the stupid stainless steel stove and fridge and how the fucking peppermint tea at their new apartment was in a green glass jar with a snap lid, one of a set of three that Sarah had bought us as a housewarming gift, and how I still had the other two, the big one and the littlest one, I kept coffee in one and that granulated unrefined sugar stuff in the other, they were still in the cupboard next to the stove at my big empty house in Drumheller. I told her about finding Allyson's secret degree, how shitty that made me feel that she had felt the need to keep that from me, how it made me feel like a wife-beater or some kind of bad man, even though I had hardly ever raised my voice at her, much less my hand. I told her details I didn't even know were in my head, until they turned into words and passed over my lips and hung there naked in the air above her desk between us.

Mostly the doctor nodded, occasionally jotting something down in her notepad. She asked me short questions, to lubricate the small spaces when I wasn't talking.

"Do you feel angry with Allyson because she left you, or because of the way she left you? The secrets, the suddenness of it all?"

"Did I say I was angry? Did I use that word? I don't remember. I've never talked this much all at once in my entire life."

"You're doing just fine, Joseph. We're almost out of time. But for your first session, you're doing great."

"Actually, this isn't half as hard as I thought it was going to be. I'm really relieved. And I feel better already. Hopefully we can wrap this whole thing up today, and I can just get a prescription for whatever I need from you and head out of here by Monday, like I planned. I really have to thank you, doctor, for seeing me on such short notice."

She smiled.

"I generally don't send patients on their way after just one session. I would like to see you again soon, in the next couple of days, and then again in the next couple of weeks. If you can't stay in town that long, or if you feel the commute is too much, I can have my assistant arrange a referral to a colleague of mine in Drumheller. You might find that more convenient."

"Tell you the truth, I'd really rather not see someone in Drumheller, if it's all the same to you. Let's just say I think I prefer the anonymity of the big city when it comes to this. No offense."

"I totally understand. You can work things out with Stephen on your way out, and he'll book your next session. In the meantime, I am going to ask you to do one thing." She opened a drawer and took out a slim black hardcover notebook and a pen, placed them on top of her desk, and pushed them towards me. "I would like you to make daily notes, for us to be able to read over and discuss in future sessions together. Just a record of the events of your days, and your thoughts on what kind of moods you find yourself in. We'll use the notes to try to figure out what kind of events or situations in your life cause you stress or anxiety, anger, depression. Write down anything you want. And I'll see you again in a couple of days."

She stood up and shook my hand. Her hand was ultra soft, and felt like how her voice sounded. Like bathroom tiles against your bare feet on a real scorcher of a summer day.

By the time I got back out to my truck, it was almost five and rush hour was in full swing. It was nearly dark, which felt a bit weird. I wasn't used to sleeping in, and it felt like the night had snuck up behind me somehow. I wasn't used to not having any real work done at the end of a day, either. Wasn't like me at all. My other unfinished business was weighing heavy on my mind.

I had an hour before I had to be back at the motel to babysit Raylene. I could try calling Allyson again, and go drop off her boxes. I wouldn't have much time to hang around and talk, which I considered a plus. But I thought I should try Cecilia again. Her place was on the other side of town and it was rush hour, but if I hauled ass I could whip over and still get back to the motel on time. I could meet with Ally first thing tomorrow morning, hopefully, and then get hold of the cello teacher. My next appointment with the shrink was Monday, early afternoon. I could have a cello lesson sometime over the weekend, get my head shrunk one more time, and be back in Drumheller by dinnertime. My mom usually made lasagna on Mondays, and I was really starting to miss my dog. The last time Buck Buck and I were separated for this long was the honeymoon, when Ally and I went to Mexico for six days. According to Franco, the poor dog refused to eat anything except raw weiners, wouldn't budge from the front door, and ate a pair of Franco's Italian leather dress shoes in protest.

The porch light at Cecelia's was on, and the door to the glass sunroom was ajar. Inside I could see there was a half-smoked cigarette in an ashtray perched on the arm of a faded loveseat. I pressed the doorbell, but didn't hear it buzz inside. I could hear a distant radio, but no footsteps. I knocked on the door, and the little dog inside went ballistic again. Then a woman's muffled call underneath it: *be right there.*

The deadbolt soon clicked, and the smell of steam and corn-on-the-cob escaped as the door swung open.

Cecelia Carson was one of the most beautiful women I ever laid my eyes upon in real life. She was wearing a men's waffled undershirt that was once white, a pair of kneeless jeans, and leather moccasins. One long braid trailed from the back of her neck over her shoulder and all the way down to her hips. That was some long hair, if she ever shook it loose. Brown feather duster eyelashes.

"Yes?"

"Hello, my name is Joseph Cooper. I'm an acquaintance of your husband, Jim. I know him from Drumheller."

"James is my brother, not my husband. I'm not married."

"My mistake, Ms Carson, I apologize." Her brother, not her husband. I stared at my feet, feeling awkward. "So a couple of days before your brother left town, he traded me his cell for a used car I had for sale."

"He gave away the cello? I can't believe that."

"Well, like I said, he didn't give it away, I traded him a car for it. Anyways, the car broke down, and he had me tow it back to my shop and fix it up for him. I fixed it right away and brought it back the next day, but your brother had left town. No forwarding address. So now I've got his car, and it's running fine, but I don't know how to get hold of him to find out what he wants me to do with it. I found your address on a postcard he left behind in his bus. So here I am."

She said nothing as she stood in the doorway, one hip leaning against the doorframe, and fiddled with the end of her braid. I shifted my weight from one foot to the other.

"Sorry." She shook her head. "I just can't get over the fact that he let go of Elaine's cello. It was in her family for years. Tell you what, I'm expecting to hear from him tomorrow, he's supposed to call here. I don't have a number I can reach him at, as usual. But I'll be sure to ask him about the car. We'll figure out what he wants to do with it. He's not that into owning much in the way of material belongings. You've probably already figured that out, if you knew him at all."

"Not really. I mean, I'd see him around here and there, I knew who he was, but I never talked to him until he came around asking about the car."

"What did he want a car for? That's not like Jim at all. You can't live in a car. Did his old bus break down?"

"No, actually, I fired it up the day I tried to drop the car off for him, and it turned right over."

I hadn't thought of that. Why the hell didn't he just do the deed in his bus? Wouldn't that have been cheaper? The bus had started up just fine.

"He left the bus behind, too?" Cecilia knit her eyebrows together and fished the half-smoked cigarette out of the ashtray by the door, felt her pockets for a lighter. I fumbled mine out of my jacket pocket and lit it for her. My hands were shaking just a little. I could smell her shampoo. I found myself trying not to look directly at her, just in case I couldn't stop.

She took a slow drag and half-sat on the arm of the loveseat. "I can't believe he left the bus, too. Now that is really weird. One of his kids was born in that little bus. When he and Elaine were in their hippie phase. He loved that thing. Had it for twenty years."

His kid was born in it. He couldn't die there. That made sense to me.

Cecelia stared at the red end of her cigarette like it might know something neither of us did. "Something is up with my brother. I'll figure it all out when he calls here tomorrow. Why don't you drop by here tomorrow night, after seven? Do you have a pen? I'll give you my number."

She crushed the butt of her smoke and stood up. I could smell her shampoo again, and it made my heart speed up. I did, indeed, have a pen, and the notebook from the doctor. I had tucked them under my arm when I got out of the truck, just in case I had to leave a note.

The very first thing I wrote in my stress journal was Cecelia Carson's phone number, and seven p.m.

"Nice to meet you, Joseph Cooper. I'll talk to you tomorrow." She waved at me and closed the door behind her.

"Nice to meet you too, Cecelia Carson," I said, and finally let out my breath.

I ended up back at the motel right at six-thirty, just as Kelly rounded the corner next to the parking lot, with Raylene and what looked like a stuffed moose in tow. Kelly's backpack was bulging with books. How much could you learn about dog grooming from a book, I wondered.

"Hey Joseph, here we are, all ready for Mommy to go to school, right, honey?"

Raylene glowered at me from under the hood of her parka.

"She always plays shy for the first little while. She'll snap out of it, won't you, honey?" Kelly tugged on Raylene's arm for an answer, but Raylene just scrunched her mouth up into a silent little knot.

I reached out to take the girl's hand, but she white-knuckled it, wouldn't let go of Kelly's. Popped the thumb of her other hand into her mouth. Kelly brushed Raylene's thumb out of her mouth with her free hand.

"No thumb, Bug. Mommy can't afford a retainer for you."

The kid screwed up her face like she was trying to squeeze out a tear, but Kelly ignored it.

"You're going to stay with Joseph for a while so I can go to school and learn how to take care of our new puppy."

"We don't have a puppy yet."

"We will, Bug, if you let me go to school."

I unlocked my door and Kelly led Raylene into my room, sat her on the chair, and took off her boots. But Raylene wouldn't let Kelly take her coat off.

"It's too cold in here."

The kid was right. It was freezing. I crossed the room and turned on the heater under the window.

"I can take her coat off for her in a minute then, once it warms up in here," I said.

"I can take my own coat off my own self," Raylene snipped, her tiny arms crossed over her chest.

"He knows you can take off your own coat, Raylene, he's just being a gentleman. You're not used to that. Don't be rude to the man, he's doing us a favour."

Kelly stood up and turned to face me. She was wearing a bit of eye shadow, and smelled like fresh nail polish. "I should head out, or I'm gonna miss my bus. Thanks a lot, Joseph, you're a real lifesaver. I talked to Lenny already, told him you were a real nice guy and that he shouldn't be ripping you off so much for this dinky little room. He told me he'd cut you a bit of a deal. Make sure he doesn't weasel out of it. I'll see you two in a few hours." Kelly opened her backpack, took out a colouring book and a zip-lock bag of crayons, put them on the unused bed. "Give Mommy a little kiss, Bug, and you be on your best behaviour for Joseph, or it's no zoo for you this weekend."

Kelly ran her hand over an errant blonde tuft of bangs that was sticking out from under the hood of Raylene's parka and leaned over as the kid tilted one cheek up, permitted it to be kissed. Kicked her feet out and let them bounce back against the legs of the chair, her thumbs folded into her fists.

And then Kelly was gone, and it was just me and Raylene, still perched on the chair in the corner. The kid kind of freaked me out a bit. One of those know-all, see-all, red rum types of kid you run into every once in a while.

Her little mittens were hanging from pink wool strings out the ends of her parka sleeves. Pink rubber boots with fake sheepskin around the top, dark pink pants, a plastic daisy bracelet around one wrist. The kid was styling, in the same way as her mother. Capri Motor Court dazzle.

"You want something to drink?'

She shook her head.

"Want to watch TV?"

She shrugged once, still silent.

"You need to go to the bathroom or anything? You want to take your coat off, or at least untie your hood?"

Another shake of her head. She stared at me. It was starting to look like it was going to be a long night, for both of us.

"Well I have to keep a journal, write down all the things I did today, so I'm going to go ahead and do that now. You can watch TV, or colour, or whatever you want. You just let me know if you need anything."

I grabbed my journal off the side table and flipped it open on the bed in front of me. On the inside of the front cover, I wrote my name, address, and phone number, in case I ever lost it. Then I thought about someone finding it, and considered crossing that information out, but I decided instead that I would never let the journal out of my sight. I turned past Cecelia's phone number to a fresh clean page. Wrote the date and time in the top left corner. Capri Motor Court, room 119 after that. Then I ran out of ideas for a minute, so I laid my pen down, and looked at the kid.

She still had her parka on, but had sat down on the other bed, cross-legged, just like I was. Her colouring book open in front of her, a black crayon poised in the air above it. She put it down when she felt me looking at her, crossed her skinny little arms over her chest again. Uncrossed them, let out a big dramatic sigh.

"I'm writing my day down, too. In a picture. I'm drawing the swing set at daycare," she informed me, all business-like.

"Good idea."

I picked up my pen again. Started to write whatever came into my head.

This must be what it's like to hang out with me sometimes. This kid makes me nervous. I thought kids were supposed to be noisy, ask a million questions, break stuff. Whatever. Raylene is stressing me out a little. She's not like my nieces at all. Chelsea and Stella would be all over this place by now, into everything. I get the feeling she doesn't like me, and I don't quite know why I care. I'm out of here on Monday, and I'll probably never see her again.

"Are you writing about babysitting me?" Raylene kept drawing right through her question, didn't look up.

"No. I haven't got to that bit yet," I lied, not sure why I was doing it.

"Tell me when you're writing about me then. I could draw you a picture of me and you to go with your story." She flipped to a clean page, smoothed it flat with one hand, the pink tip of her tongue poking out one side of her mouth. She was cute when she wasn't scowling at something.

"That's a great idea, Raylene. I would like that a lot." For some reason this tugged at my chest a little, like when one of my nieces wrapped their little monkey arms around my neck, or jumped up and down when I came through their front door. She was warming up to me. Just liked to take her time about it. I could respect that.

"Do you want me to put my momma in the picture too?"

"Whatever you like, Raylene, it's your picture. You're the artist here."

"But I'm making it for you."

"Well, my story is about me babysitting you, so I guess it should be a picture of just you and me, if it's going to go with my story."

"I thought you weren't writing that part yet."

There wasn't much that got past this kid.

"Well, I'm just getting there now."

Raylene eyed me for a long second, and exchanged her black crayon for a yellow one.

"Do you want to kiss her?"

"Do I want to kiss who?"

"My momma, stupid head."

Did the kid just call me stupid head?

"I don't want to kiss your mommy. We're just friends, is all. She's a really nice person, but I'm way to old to be kissing her."

"Mr Big Ass is even older than you, and he wants to kiss my mom all the time."

I laughed out loud at that one. "I bet he does. Who is Mr Big Ass?"

"The man who lives here all the time. He takes our money so we can stay here. My mom says he has eight arms and wants to kiss her. But I want her to kiss you instead of him."

That fucking Lenny. I thought of his hairy hands, his shrunken wife coming around here every morning, cleaning out my little trash can, talking to me about the weather, asking if I need clean towels. I felt like hitting him. I picked my pen up again.

Some guys make me ashamed of my species. Kelly's just a kid, and she is vulnerable. Some guys are like hyenas, or wolves. They always go after the injured ones, the limping. The ones who have fallen behind the pack a little.

"Hey, Raylene? I think I changed my mind. I think you should put your mom in the picture after all. Just don't draw us so we're kissing."

Raylene sat up straight, reached for a different crayon. Her face split into a quick smile, then settled back into serious concentration. "I'm going to make her wearing a pretty dress then. A new one, for special."

We hung out like that for a while, chatting and drawing and writing. Raylene finally announced to me that her picture was done, and could I untie her hood for her. I slipped her out of her parka and she curled up under the covers of the other bed, her stuffed moose tucked up under her chin.

"You can put the TV on if you want," she said. "I can sleep even through a lot of noises." Soon after, she crashed right out. I nodded off too at some point, on top of the sheets with my boots still on. The eleven o'clock news was on when Kelly woke me up with a soft knock on the door. Raylene was snoring, a lot louder than I thought a little girl could. I let Kelly in, and she sat on the edge of Raylene's bed, her cheeks red from the cold, her hand absentmindedly stroking her daughter's foot through the covers.

"Was she good? She looks so innocent when she's asleep. You'd never know by looking at her now, how bad she can be if she feels like it."

"She was a perfect angel. She drew me a picture, and then passed out around eight or so. We had a good time. She's a smart kid. I like her a lot."

"Well, I guess I should pack her up and get myself to bed. I'm opening tomorrow, at six."

"What do you do with Raylene that early? Is her day-care open all weekend, too?"

Kelly shook her head. "I take her with me on Saturdays. She likes it. She helps me straighten out the chip bags and stuff, put the paper towels in. My friend Dianne picks her up on her way to work at eight and drops Raylene and her daughter off at her Grandma's place on weekends. Sometimes I babysit for Dianne as a favour back, if she has to work late or something."

"Sounds complicated."

"You gotta do what you gotta do."

"Well, I'm around till Monday afternoon, at least, if you need a hand with her again. She's no trouble at all."

"You're so nice to us, Joseph. You still gonna come by for pork chops on Sunday?"

"Wouldn't miss it."

Kelly pulled the covers off Raylene, who didn't move a hair. I picked her up; she was damp with sweat and her small shape radiated heat like a barbecue briquette. Kelly slung her onto her hip, picked up her backpack with her other hand.

"Could you toss that bag of crayons in here, Joseph? Raylene probably wants you to keep the drawing. She always does."

Kelly left, mouthing a silent good night to me, Raylene still not lifting an eyelid. I took the drawing and studied it for a minute before tucking it between two empty pages of my stress journal. Raylene had drawn all three of us in a neat row. A quarter of a yellow sun hung in the top corner of the page, its orange rays touching our perfectly round heads. Her mother smiling with cherry red lips, and a light blue triangle for a dress, complete with a smoking cigarette that dangled between two of her three oversized fingers. Raylene in the middle, her triangle dress purple to match her shoes. The image of me was huge, way out of proportion to her and her mother. She had written my name under her stick rendition of me, spelled with an f on the end. Just like it sounded.

I was up and showered by seven o'clock the next morning, wide awake and ready to go. I couldn't believe it, but I was actually missing the feeling of getting my hands dirty.

I could hear Hector moving around next door, flushing his toilet, the bang of water running through old plumbing. I wondered if he would mind if I started in on the cello this early. I didn't have that much to do with myself.

I opened up my stress journal.

7:06 a.m. Trying to relax stresses me out. I work so much because most of the time I don't know where to put my hands. Maybe that is why I can't quit smoking.

Maybe I could take Hector out for breakfast. I picked up the phone to call him, instead of just knocking. Maybe he wasn't decent yet.

"Good morning, Hector McHugh residence."

"Hector. It's Joseph. Can I take you out to breakfast? I heard you up over there. Hope it's not to early to call."

"Not at all, my friend. In fact, it's the best time of the day. I'll be over in a minute or so."

I went to put my journal away in the bureau drawer, but thought again. I should keep it with me. Hector would understand. I could tell him I was writing a book, too. Or I could tell him nothing. Fuck it, I could tell him it was my stress journal. He'd made his own hair fall out from stress, he'd told me so. Maybe Hector already knew all about stress journals.

Hector rapped three times on the door, then opened it

himself. He smelled like soap, and like aftershave, but not the obnoxious stuff. Kind of woody like.

"You got a favourite place you like for breakfast? I'm buying this time."

"Do you like crepes?"

"Never had them, I don't think."

"What a tragedy. We can take my truck."

Hector drove me to a tiny little house converted into a restaurant, with a picket fence around a deck and sparse winter garden. It smelled amazing inside, a combination of coffee and cakes in the oven. When the waitress came, Hector ordered for both of us without even opening the menu.

"Two Americanos with steamed milk, and two apple and cheddar crepes, please. Thank you, Bernie."

"Sure thing, Hector. And this one's name is...?"

I remembered the ladder-boned cowboy from a couple nights ago. "My name is Joseph."

"Hector has the best-looking friends, I swear." She winked at me and disappeared into the back. I felt the red warm the back of my neck, and Hector smiled.

"I believe she's taken a fancy to you, Joseph."

"She probably talks to all the guys like that. Make more tips."

"She's actually not like that at all. She's the daughter of an old friend of mine. I've known her since she was a baby. Bernadette. She's both the cook and the server here."

"I'm sorry Hector. No offense. I didn't know you were friends."

"I'm her godfather." There was a twinkle in his eye. "I'm trying to set the two of you up, to be quite honest. I was already thinking of asking you here for breakfast when you called. She's long past due to meet a decent guy, and if you don't mind me saying so, Joseph, you've got lonely all over you, and I thought you two might hit it off. I told her about your cello. I hope you'll forgive me for meddling, but I wanted her to meet you." Hector whispered this last bit, looking past me over my shoulder.

Bernadette appeared with two sturdy mugs of coffee and raised a sly eyebrow at Hector, then disappeared back through the swinging doors of the kitchen.

I leaned forward across the table, keeping my voice down. "I'm very flattered, Hector, believe me, but I don't think I'm good dating material right now, if you know what I mean. I'm having panic attacks. I have to keep a stress journal. I'm supposed to be taking things easy. Avoiding stimulants." I spooned sugar into my coffee, shaking my head at myself.

"I just thought a bit of female attention might do you some good."

"The last thing I need is more women in my life, Hector. My wife is a lesbian, and my mother is a pit bull."

"All the more reason to meet a new woman, if you ask me. Reacquaint yourself with the benefits of the fairer sex."

Bernadette appeared with our breakfasts, and Hector fell silent, his eyes focused on the beautiful plate she placed front of him. Three perfect crepes, steaming under a light cheese sauce, fresh herbs on the top, a fan of fresh fruit and parsley.

"Bernadette, you are an artist."

"Eat your breakfast, old man. Call me if you need more coffee. I'm making a soufflé and have to keep an eye on it. I'll come chat when it's out of the oven."

It was the best breakfast I ever had and I ate every scrap

of it, would have licked the plate if I were home alone. Hector ate his in an orderly fashion, cutting it into careful bites. I finished way before he did, and found myself eyeing his plate.

"You could order yourself another, if you're still hungry."

"Sorry. That was the most delicious thing I think I ever ate."

"Maybe you should think again about asking her on a date."

"I can't just ask someone out because I like her cooking. That wouldn't be right."

"You see, that is why I want you to go out with her. You're a good man."

"I'm a mess."

"Who isn't?"

I changed the subject. "How long were you and your wife together before she died?"

Hector sipped his coffee. "Thirty-two years. I married her when I was twenty, and she died on my fifty-second birthday. Almost eleven years ago. She was fifty-four. Overdosed on painkillers. She had been losing a long argument with cancer for several years. She was in a lot of pain. Some might call it suicide, she would call it bowing out gracefully."

"I'm really sorry, Hector, I shouldn't have asked. It's none of my business."

"I don't mind at all, it was a long time ago now. I can't expect you to do all of the talking. Wouldn't be much of a conversation then, would it?"

"My mom said pretty much the same thing to me a couple of days ago."

"Your mother sounds like a smart woman."

Bernadette came out, wiping her hands on a clean rag, and sat down next to Hector.

"Breakfast was perfect, as usual," Hector said. "I had to fight Joseph off to keep him from eating mine as well."

Bernadette smiled at me. "Where did you meet this old rascal then?"

"We're both staying at the Capri. We're neighbours. I actually live in Drumheller."

"I love that town. I drive out to the Hoodoos all the time. I should look you up next time I'm through. Does Hector have your number there?"

"I'll make sure I leave it with him. What do we owe you for breakfast? I'm buying."

"It's on me. Hector's helped me out a lot. The least I can do is feed his friends crepes."

"Well, thank you very much. It was the best breakfast I ever had."

"You probably say that to all the ladies."

"No." I said. "I've never had crepes before today."

Bernadette then looked at me with the same direct gaze as Hector. "It was nice to meet you, Joseph. Come by any time. This guy's here almost every morning."

Hector kissed Bernadette on both cheeks, and didn't say anything until we were back in his truck.

"She's a lovely young woman, no? She had a bad experience with her last beau, who was heavy-handed with her. She hasn't really dated since. The whole experience left her a bit gun-shy."

"She doesn't seem like the type of woman who would put up with any bullshit," I said.

"There is no type of woman that allows a man to hit her.

There is only the type of man that would beat his wife."

"I guess. I just can't imagine anyone hitting a woman like that and getting away with it."

"What makes you think he got away with it? Don't delude yourself into thinking women are the weaker sex, Joseph. They are just expected to tolerate more bullshit than we are."

"You go to college, Hector? You talk like a professor sometimes."

Hector shook his head. "I went to work in the bush as soon as I got through with high school. Driving a bulldozer for the government, fixing up the Alaska Highway. They had built it in such a panic during the war, because of the Japanese threat. I met my wife in Dawson Creek, she was a waitress in her father's restaurant. I was just a grunt at the time, but after two summers of overtime, I went back there and asked her to marry me. I had saved up for a truck and started my own little business, supplying mining camps all over the north with food and parts, stuff like that. We had good fun together, working like dogs all summer and then travelling five or so months out of the year, spending our winters all over the world."

"You never had kids?"

"No. Anna was an exceptional woman, very strong-minded. She wanted a different life than her mother's, or any of the other women she knew. We read books, we travelled, we dined. We did whatever we wanted. People with children are not usually afforded those kinds of freedoms. Especially women. Anna believed childbirth was largely responsible for the enslavement of women."

"You never wanted a son? Pass on the family name, all that stuff?"

Hector shrugged. "I guess I never felt it was for me to decide, lacking a womb, as I do."

"Sounds like you two were kind of radical."

"If a marriage between two equals seems radical to you, then I guess we were."

"I meant for forty years ago. Ally and I were kind of like that, too. Equals. We did our own things. We never had kids, but that was only because I lack the necessary sperm count."

Before we knew it, we had arrived back at the Capri. Hector turned the engine off and turned to look at me.

"So how do you feel about that?"

"I was pretty bummed about it, actually. I really wanted kids, like, three of them, but Ally wanted to start with just one, and see how it went. I was heartbroken when I first found out. Deep blue funk, even. At first I blamed my sperm count when she left me for Kathleen, which is ironic, if you think about it. But now I watch Kelly with Raylene, and how my sister thinks she can't leave the dink she married because of her two daughters, and I try to imagine how much harder my divorce would have been, you know, with a baby in the picture. How I'd feel only seeing my kid on weekends and every other Christmas, and having to watch someone else raise them up, like some of my buddies have to. Then I think maybe I'm grateful. Raising kids seems a lot more complicated than it used to be."

"I think the very same thing all the time. Evidence of it everywhere."

We sat there in the truck for another second or two, just staring through the windshield at the empty swimming pool.

"I should be off," Hector said finally. "I've got a few errands to do."

"Me too. Take care of yourself, Hector. I'll talk to you later."

I stood outside my door, watching Hector back his truck out and leave. He raised four fingers at me to wave goodbye, keeping his thumb and the palm of his hand on the steering wheel. My dad used to do the very same thing.

I sat down on the edge of my bed, my journal open in front of me.

9:15 a.m. Even the thought of dating anyone stresses me out. It makes me feel broken, just thinking about it. Like I'm missing a wheel, or my transmission won't let me shift out of reverse. Like I got taken apart and put back together again, but missing a few pieces.

Seeing Allyson again stresses me out. She seems like she's morphed into some whole new person, but I'm still here, just being who I've always been. Treading water, with all these questions I need answers to. Except the person I want to ask isn't around anymore.

I closed the book and picked up the phone.

Just when I thought I was going to get her machine again, Allyson picked up on the third ring.

"Joseph! How come you didn't call me yesterday? Have you checked in with your mother?"

"Aren't you going to ask me how I'm doing?"

"I was just getting to that. Did you call that doctor yet?"

"I already had my first session. I'm all over it."

"Your first session? Is this going to be a regular thing? Like Tony Soprano?"

"Who?"

"He's a television character, Joey. A mafia crime boss."

"What does that have to do with me?"

"He goes to a shrink, Joseph, pay attention. He goes

every week. Is that what you're going to have to do? That's going to be a lot of driving, isn't it? There must be a shrink in Drumheller, the place is full of nut cases."

"I like this doctor. Besides, if there's a shrink in Drumheller, chances are I play hockey with him, or I went to school with his wife or some fucking thing. The drive is worth it. Plus, I'm lining up a cello teacher in Calgary. I'm going to take some lessons. Did I tell you I got myself a cello?"

"Your mom told me. But I think she thinks it's a viola. A cello makes more sense."

"What is that supposed to mean?"

"I can barely imagine you playing the cello, much less a viola, Joey. That's what it means. You listen to classic rock, is all. I would have thought maybe the electric guitar, or something."

"Rick Davis says any dumbfuck can learn to play 'Stairway to Heaven' on the electric guitar. He says the cello is classy. That chicks will dig it."

"Rick might just be right. I'd like to hear you play the cello sometime."

"Not any time soon. All I can play is the first bit of 'I Found My Thrill on Blueberry Hill.'"

"Your dad used to love that song, remember?"

"I think that's why I picked that song to learn. So what are you up to this morning? Can I come by and drop off these boxes?"

"Only if you let me take you out for breakfast."

"I just finished breakfast with my buddy from next door."

"Coffee, then."

"I'm supposed to be avoiding stimulants."

"Then I'll buy you a juice. You know what I mean, Joey. Don't you think we should maybe … hang out, just you and me? Kathleen is at yoga, and then she's working all afternoon."

"What's she do?"

"She works in a group home for high-risk kids. She takes them on field trips, does workshops, counselling, stuff like that."

"I like her, she seems nice."

Allyson was silent for a minute.

"Come on over, Joey. We can talk face to face, just you and me. I'd really like that."

"You want me to bring anything?"

"Just you."

I hung up. Opened up my journal again.

9:30 a.m. On my way over to meet with Ally. She told me just to bring myself. She used to say that all the time, when I'd call her just before I left work to come home. Do you need anything? All I need right now is you, she would say.

Stress level: medium, with periods of a slow high. Weather: overcast. Mood: vaguely depressed, giving way to reluctant hope in the late afternoon.

Before I left, I kind of uncharacteristically took a swig out of the bottle of scotch Hector had left on the desk, then brushed my teeth, so it would just be my little secret. Didn't want Ally leaking it to my mom that I was hitting the sauce.

When I arrived, Ally was wearing a pair of blue yoga pants and one of my old shirts, still in her bare feet. I had forgot all about that old shirt. It was corduroy, kind of a suede colour, with pearly snaps. I loved that shirt. I was trying to feel pissed off that Ally had boosted it from me, but the truth was I had forgotten to miss it. Then I got to thinking for a second about Ally wearing my shirt to bed with someone else pressed up against her, and I chased the topic from my mind, because I could feel it starting to make my heart race a little. It occurred to me that hanging out in their love nest might be negatively affecting my mental health. Probably got blood on their hardwood floors the last time I visited.

"Why are you shaking your head, Joey? You want to go unload my stuff or not? I'd love to help, but you're standing on my shoes."

I was standing like a dumbfuck, parked like a deep freeze in the middle of her doorway, my tongue stuck to the roof of my mouth. I swallowed and looked down. She was right. I passed Ally her runners, the sweat socks balled up inside of them.

"I parked right out back, close to the elevator. We can drag them that far. They're pretty heavy, like I said."

"Thanks again for bringing my stuff."

"I wasn't fishing for thank you's, Ally. Be careful of your back when you start lifting the boxes."

"I'm thanking you because I mean it, really. I'm sorry I didn't come and get it all sooner. Besides, you're the one whose back is shot."

"It doesn't bug me so much as it used to. All that yoga you forced on me helped, after all."

"I told you so."

"You did so. Mostly I didn't like going because Franco kept giving me a hard time. Nine thousand jokes about me wearing tights. It got a little tired. I tried telling him how yoga class was just me and twenty really flexible women, but he wouldn't listen."

156

"You care too much what people think."

"Let's go move some boxes."

"I'm serious, Joey. It's bad for your health."

"Don't you have a new wife to nag?"

Allyson stopped short. "Are you trying to be an asshole?"

"It just comes to me naturally."

"You're starting to sound like your father."

"Thank you."

Ally slapped my arm, right where my shirtsleeve was rolled up to. "Smartass."

"You're not allowed to beat me anymore."

"Don't let Kathleen hear you talk like that. She volunteers for a shelter hotline."

"Kidding. Besides, you started it."

We went on like that while we got her stuff out of my truck into the elevator, dragged it down the hallway, and stashed it in the little office space under the loft. About nothing and everything.

"Have a seat, I'll put the kettle on for us," Ally said when we were done. "Take off your coat. I want to talk to you about something."

Sit down, I want to talk to you about something. What happened the last time she said something like that to me? I mentally reached for my stress journal, remembered it was sitting on the front seat of my truck, the pen clipped to its front cover.

I sat down in the armchair but kept my jacket on.

Ally brought us some tea. Chamomile. Thank Christ, I thought. Anything but peppermint. At least this time if I passed out I was already sitting in an armchair, and wouldn't knock myself out.

Ally sat on the couch, her feet tucked underneath her.

"So tell me how your life is these days. I mean, I get the bare facts from your mom, but I want details."

"I've been all right. Fair to middling, I'd say. Better lately. Aside from a panic attack and the stitches in my head, I'd say this little vacation's been real good to me. I'm looking forward to my cello lesson. I like playing the thing, a lot more than I thought. Gives me something to do."

"We should jam sometime. Give me an excuse to dust off my oboe. Haven't touched it since we got this place. I'm mostly into taking pictures now, and stuff for school. I'm taking a textile course, a darkroom class, some computer stuff. I love going to school. I need the discipline. I never seem to get much done without a deadline."

This would have been the ideal opportunity for me to ask her about her Master's degree, and if it was anything I did that made her feel like she couldn't tell me she wanted to go back to school, but I rolled all my questions around in the back of my mouth, then swallowed them. Washed them down with herbal tea. We were getting along so well. The past was done. I missed her, and just wanted to talk, didn't want to get all heavy. I looked at my watch.

10:25 a.m. Talking to my ex-wife about why she left stresses me out so much I avoid it at all costs. Even though it might help if I knew.

I wrote it down in my head, for later.

"You need to be somewhere? That's the third time you've looked at your watch in the last twenty minutes."

"Sorry, Al. Force of habit. I bill out by the hour. This is only my fifth day off, and I don't know what to do with my hands. I think maybe I'm a workaholic."

158

"You're just figuring that out now?"

"Better late than never, right?"

Allyson shifted around on the couch. I could tell she was about to change the subject.

"Speaking of which, I have something I need to tell you. Kathleen and I ... we're having a baby."

"Both of you?"

"We're a couple."

"I know that, Allyson. I mean, which one of you is pregnant?"

"Kathleen is. I couldn't face all that again, the pee tests, the ovulating calendar. She's thirty-six, and she really misses Mitch's kids. She's always wanted kids of her own."

10:35 a.m. My wife is having a lesbian love child. And for some reason this also stresses me out.

"Can I ask who the daddy is?" I wasn't quite sure I wanted to know, but on the other hand, I didn't want to be the only one who didn't know.

"The donor. We did it by artificial insemination. He's married, an old friend of Kathleen's. Nice guy."

"How do they do that exactly? Did she have to go to the hospital to get it done?"

"Do you really want to know the how and where?"

"Probably not, actually."

"I didn't think so."

We sat there for a minute, staring into our teacups.

"So how do you feel about this, Joseph?"

She hardly ever called me Joseph.

"How am I supposed to feel? You just told me five seconds ago. It wasn't exactly on my list of things I thought were gonna happen. No offense, but it's like me taking up the cello. Who would have seen that one coming? I guess the first thing it makes me feel is like I have a low sperm count. Like I'm a lemon. A recallable model."

"Well, that's actually what I wanted to talk to you about. What Kathleen and I were going to talk to you about the other day. We want to ask you if you would consider being a part of our child's life. You're my family, Joey, and so is Ruth. Even Sarah. You always will be. I was an only child, a lonely one, you know that. I want something different for my kid. I want him or her to have a real family. A grandma. I don't even remember what my mom looked like, except from pictures. And I know how much you want to be a father. I've thought about it a lot. I want you to be our baby's co-parent."

"What about Kathleen? What does she think about all this?"

"She feels the same way. We've talked about it quite a bit. Ruth is all for it, too. She's already making a quilt."

"My mom knows about all this? Jesus fuck me, why am I always the last one to get told about everything? I had a heart to heart with her just the other day, and she didn't breathe a word about any of this."

"I asked her to let me tell you when you came to town. Face to face."

"What does being a co-parent mean, exactly?"

"It means we want the baby to have a father, and we want it to be you."

I took a deep breath and sunk deeper into the armchair. There was a time when the thing I wanted most in the world was to raise up a baby with Allyson. I just never imagined this was what it would look like.

"What about the … sperm guy? How does he feel about having me around his kid?"

"It won't be his kid. He already has a family. He agreed to be our donor, not a father. We're asking you. I always said you would make a great daddy, and I still think that."

"Can I think about it?"

"You can take the next seven months to think about it. It's not like we have anyone else lined up. It's not like that."

"I'm really flattered, Ally. Kind of blown away, to be honest. I need to think about it, though. I was just trying to get over the fact I wasn't ever going to be anyone's dad. It's a bit much for me to wrap my head around, all at once."

"Take your time. Whatever time you need."

I shook my head, trying to bend it around all of what she was really asking me. "So say I was the kid's father, and obviously Kathleen would be the mother, then what is it going to call you?"

"Allyson? Maybe mom, too. We'll figure that out when we need to. We'll let the kid decide." She was leaning forward now, her eyes bright.

"I wonder what my dad would have to say about all this."

"He would have loved being a grandpa, and you know it. But I'm not asking your dad, I'm asking you. I only ever really had the one parent, Joey, and he was never much of a father. I would have given everything to have a mother, and this baby will have two. Three parents would be even better."

"My buddy Hector was just saying this morning that not having children gave you more freedom. His wife thought childbirth enslaved women. What does that mean for lesbian parents?"

"It's the patriarchal concept of the nuclear family that keeps people stuck in the system, not the act of child-rearing itself. It takes a village to raise a true villager."

I looked at her sideways. "Did you learn that in art school?"

"Simone de Beauvoir, I think it was. Or maybe it was Hillary Clinton, I can't remember."

The sun slanted in wide beams through the window behind her. She looked good with short hair. I hugged her before I left, and she hugged me back, long and hard.

It wasn't until I got outside the building and the wind hit my face that I realized I was crying. What the fuck was up with me?

10:40 a.m. Allyson just asked me to co-parent the baby her girlfriend is going to have. A three-way family unit. I'm already hoping it's a boy, I must admit. Three women might be a little too much for me to deal with. A son. I could teach him how to fix cars. Only if he wants to, though. Fuck it, I could teach him how to play the cello.

Stress level: surprisingly low, all things considered. Weather: periodic sunny breaks. Mood: elated, like a brand new father.

I wrote with the book open in my lap in the cab of my truck, then drove straight back to the motel. Hector's truck was missing from the parking lot. I went to my room to see if I had a message from the cello lady.

Caroline had called me back. Lenny's wife answered the phone at the front desk and gave me the message. I was extra nice to her on the phone, since I now knew what a bastard her husband was.

I called Caroline right away.

"Caroline here."

"Hi, it's Joseph Cooper here. I got your number from Rupert, the uh, percussion guy at the music store? I'm looking for cello lessons. The beginner kind."

"Hi, Joseph. What do you need to know?"

"Well, are you available over this weekend? I'm from Drumheller, and going back Monday."

"You don't want to ask me about my credentials?"

"Do you know how to play the cello?"

"Of course I do."

"And can you teach me how to play?"

She let out a laugh. "Of course I can. I teach little kids in the youth orchestra."

"Well, perfect then. That's about my skill level, too. How much you want me to pay you?"

"Thirty bucks an hour?"

Not even half of what I charge, I thought. "Sounds good to me. How about tomorrow afternoon?"

"Come to my house at three. You got a pen?"

I wrote down the address of Caroline Daws, my new cello teacher, on the first page of my stress journal, right underneath the phone number of Cecelia Carson.

"What should I bring?"

"Just yourself and your cello."

I hung up the phone, noticed my hands were sweating.

1 p.m. I now have a cello teacher. And I think I'm going to be a father. Spermless me is getting a second chance.

Stress level: minimal to none, just a bit of nerves about my first lesson. Weather: it's cold in my motel room. Mood: the last time I can remember feeling anything even close to this was the time I got my first dirt bike, the two-stroke, the summer I turned eleven. It's something like that, that's as close as I can get. I'd have to call it some kind of bliss.

I closed my stress journal. So far, the thing was really working.

I took out my cello and the library books. The tuning

fork. Flipped to the first couple pages of *How To Play a Stringed Instrument*, to ascertain once and for all just exactly how to tune the thing. I didn't want to show up on Caroline's doorstep totally clueless.

I started with the A string, just like the book told me to. It didn't take me as long as I thought. Just had to feel around for it with my ears, finding the right place for the tuning peg to sit, the note, that place that made the right colour ring inside my head.

A fifth above, or a fourth below, depending on how you looked at it, the book told me. I could feel when it sounded good when I tuned the next string to the first. Like putting the roof on a house that I had just finished framing. Like finding the value of x in algebra class. I could feel my lips relax back into my face when I got it sounding right.

I put the TV on and turned it to the public broadcasting channel again, hoping for another Bollywood movie, but instead there was a yodeling program on, which I found impossible to play along with. Picked up the book again. C-G-D-A. Those were the names of the strings. Cats Go Down Alleys, it said, a rhyme to help remember it.

C-G-D-A.

I wrote it down on a clean page so I wouldn't have to bring a kids' cello book in a clear plastic library jacket with me to my lesson tomorrow. Then I drew a sketch of my own cello, more detailed than the one in the book, with shading and shadows, and the names of all the bits, and little lines pointing, like in a parts catalogue or repair manual.

Scroll, nut, neck. Fingerboard, belly, bridge. Ribs, back, sides, and tailpiece. F holes, used to increase the resonance of the instrument's body.

Like parts of a body. All the good ones.

The name cello is an abbreviation of the Italian violon-cello, which means 'little violone.'

The violone is an obsolete instrument, a large viol, similar to a modern double bass.

I copied it straight out of my library book.

Tuned exactly one octave below the viola.

Whatever that means, I thought, but didn't write it down. The little tin of wax stuff turned out to be rosin.

Rosin allows the horsehair on the bow to grip the strings, increasing their resonance. Apply rosin with short strokes to the hair near the frog. Then apply rosin with longer strokes to the full length of the bow. The frog is the part of the bow one holds. Proper bow grip is the first thing you need to establish before continuing.

I grabbed my bow by the frog and rosined it up.

You should never touch the bow hair with your fingers (except near the frog, when the fingers may contact the hair in normal playing position), and never touch the cello strings in the area where the bow is applied to them. Even when you've just washed your hands, there is oil on the surface of your fingers. This oil will prevent proper adhesion between the bow and the string, resulting in a loss of tone.

Problems: if the fingerboard, sound post, or bridge comes loose or breaks, or if you find cracks or openings, loosen the strings right away and take it to the violin shop. If the strings buzz or dig deeply into the bridge, or feel too high or too low, take it to the violin shop. Never glue anything yourself and certainly not the bridge or sound post!

Move fine-tuning pegs by turning between thumb and forefinger, counterclockwise if sharp, clockwise if flat.

To me, sharp sounded sour, and flat sounded lukewarm. I drew the bow towards me, across the first two strings at the same time. This time they sounded dark and basement and solid. I loved how it felt, like a bottom-feeding live thing bellowing between my legs. But only if I got everything right, all at the same time. When I got it to work, I could feel my face split into a smile all on its own, like the cello was humming the bummed-out right out of me.

Vibrato.

I wrote it down because I liked the sound of the word.

Arpeggio. Do not ever lie the cello on its back on the floor. Put it on its side if you must lay it down outside of its case.

I plonked and bowed and whined around on the thing until a weird muscle under my shoulder that I never felt before began to sing in protest, and my right knee started to quake uncontrollably.

Then came Hector's efficient triple rap at my door.

"Hello, Joseph. I haven't interrupted you in a moment of inspiration, have I? I can come back if I have."

"No, Hector, as a matter of fact, you're just the man I wanted to see."

I stashed my cello away in its case, grabbed my smokes out of my coat. Hector followed me to our little bench outside.

Stress level: none, except for thinking about the kid's college fund. Weather outside: cloud cover disappearing by the early afternoon, giving way to a mix of sunny disposition mixed with periodic precipitation. Mood: never better, at least in the last year.

I closed the book in my lap. Hector was looking at me.

He didn't say anything, but I could tell he wanted to ask.

"Sorry. Just making notes in my stress journal."

Hector sat back, waited for me to continue.

"For the shrink. She thinks it will keep me off the Prozac maybe, or whatever."

"Am I causing you stress?"

"Not at all, Hector."

"Glad to hear it. I keep a journal myself. Not as regular as I should, but I've kept it up over the years. A history of my travels, the names of the people I meet, things like that. Because you forget. You really do. That was the one thing about growing old that really snuck up on me. I thought I would always remember the things that really mattered. But that is not what happened at all. Some things I just forgot."

Hector pulled out his tobacco pouch from the inside pocket of his suede coat.

A gentleman carries his wallet in his inside pocket. My dad used to tell me stuff like that when I was a teenager and he was fixing my tie or explaining the finer points of cufflinks. *Only the hired help keep their wallets in their hind pockets.* Kind of ironic, I used to think, coming from a man with permanent grease worked into the cracks in his hands. *Always keep a clean handkerchief in your pocket. You never know.*

Hector rolled a perfectly uniform cigarette and tossed it up, caught it between his lips. Bet he knew a couple Zippo tricks, too, I thought. I leaned over and cupped a hand against the wind as I lit his cigarette for him. "I just had a visit with the ex-wife."

"It looks like you survived."

"Well, Allyson had some pretty big news for me. Her and Kathleen are going to have a baby."

"Both of them?"

"Now you see, that's what I asked too. Just Kathleen. Two months along."

"Are congratulations in order then? Or is her news unplanned, or unwanted?"

"They're lesbians, Hector. They don't get pregnant by accident. I don't think."

"Well, a guy shouldn't assume anything these days."

"True enough. Anyways, they planned it all out, I guess, because they did the artificial insemination thing." I paused. "And they want me to co-parent."

Hector blew smoke up into the sky around him.

"I thought you said the young lady was already two months along."

"That's the sperm bit, Hector, the part I can't do, unfortunately. That's already been taken care of. They want me to father the kid. Like, be a father. To it. With them. The three of us."

"I see."

"Not a sexual thing. A raise-up-the-kid-together thing."

"I understand."

"So spill it, Hector. What do you think? I told Ally I need to think about it. I'm asking your honest opinion."

"The only opinion you should be concerned with is your own. You have fallen upon interesting times, Joseph. A very untraditional conundrum. What's a man to do? It's not as though you can ask your priest for guidance."

"You don't think God would frown on this, do you?"

"Don't be ridiculous. God has already done his work

– conception. Your only question should be the one you ask yourself: are you ready for this responsibility? Because you are in the rather unusual position of being able to choose. You wouldn't be abandoning the child if you were to say no. The whole arrangement seems far more civilized than how we managed these things in my day."

"Do you think it would be hard on the kid, though? To have three parents?"

"Right away I think about Kelly and Raylene, it seems so obvious. I can only imagine three parents are better than one, when it comes to the child. And to the woman who actually bears it, now that I think of it. But the important thing is what you want, Joseph. Allyson and the child's mother have already cast their stones. This next bit is totally up to you, depending on what you want."

"All I wanted since I met Ally was to raise a kid with her. To be a family."

"Then it looks as though you might get that chance after all."

"I didn't imagine it going down quite like this."

"Maybe you should have been more specific."

"Careful what you ask for, huh?"

"Indeed."

"So I believe I'm going to be a daddy, Hector. What do you think about that?"

"You want the truth?"

"That's what I'm asking."

"I think it's about as romantic as a snowstorm."

"Are snowstorms romantic?"

Hector threw the butt of his smoke on the concrete where his boot could get it, then exhaled over his shoulder.

"They certainly can be. If you come prepared for the weather."

"I think I'm going to have to buy myself a station wagon."

Hector smiled, put one hand on my shoulder. "That would probably be best."

I knocked on Cecelia Carson's front door just after seven o'clock that night. I had showered and tried to steam the crease back into my good wool pants. Wore the blue shirt Sarah got me for my birthday that last summer, with the French cuffs. She said they were all the rage again. Dad's mother-of-pearl cufflinks. I realized while I was buttoning up the collar that it was the first time I had actually put it on, which meant I hadn't been dressed up enough to wear my new shirt since August, when I turned forty.

"Joseph. You look handsome. What's the occasion?"

"I was out to dinner." Which technically wasn't a lie. I had stopped at a drive-thru on my way over. Chicken tacos. I had dressed up for chicken tacos.

"Too bad. I just made way too much pasta. I can't seem to scale the recipe down when the kids aren't here. You should come in. James hasn't called yet, but I'm expecting the phone to ring any minute. Can I pour you a glass of wine? A beer?"

"Sure."

"One of each?" Cecelia raised an eyebrow at me.

"Whatever you're having is fine, thanks."

She poured me a glass of red and passed it to me, then went to stir a pot on the stove. Smelled like fresh basil. The light on her back porch was on, shining through her fogged-up kitchen windows. I sat down at the kitchen table, which was made from a thick crosscut of pine, once varnished but now worn and scuffed. There were crayon marks on the wall between the tabletop and the window that looked out over the backyard. A battered white Toyota Corolla in the carport, alongside two street-hockey nets. A tangle of bicycles.

"Your kids are away?"

"From Friday night until I pick them up after school on Monday. They go to Seth's dad's place in Canmore. You just missed meeting them last night."

"How old are they?"

"Seth just turned twelve. Isaac will be ten in January. There they both are, on the fridge."

The fridge was a cluster of tempera paintings, pipe cleaners glued in the shape of a heart to red construction paper, and lots of photographs. Cecelia and two cotton-haired boys lined up like a row of peas in a canoe, grinning. A third kid perched in the bow, a little girl with a snarl of copper curls, holding up a dandelion, triumphant-like.

"Which one is Seth?"

"The one in the red and blue shirt."

"So Isaac is the little guy on the left?"

"That's Aiden, my ex-husband's other son. Seth's half brother. Isaac is the one with the curls. Holding the flower. That picture is from a couple years ago. He made me cut his hair off when he started grade one."

"Real cute kids."

The phone rang. Cecelia searched through the newspapers on the counter for the cordless. Caught it on the third ring.

"Hello? Hi, James. Let me take you into the other room for a minute, okay? You won't believe who's here." She pulled the phone away from her ear. "Joseph, hang tight while I talk family stuff with my brother for a minute, okay? Help yourself to some more wine if you want."

Cecelia padded down the hall, taking the phone into the front room.

I stared at my thumbs, waiting. The motor on the fridge kicked in with a buzz, drowning out the murmurs from down the hall.

Do I tell this woman what I know about her brother? Does he need her help? Does he need mine? My possible moral obligations to his suicidal tendencies kind of stress me out. After all, I did give him the car.

Stress: yes. Weather: chance of fog. Mood: strangely horny, for a change.

Cecilia was gone long enough that I started feeling weird, sitting alone at the table of a stranger. I wondered what James was going to say about me. Finally she came back and sat down across from me.

"James wants to know if you would mind towing the car into Calgary. He wants to give it to me, since my car is on its last legs. I would pay you for your time and gas."

"No need for that. I'm going to be coming back to Calgary anyways, end of next week."

"You got yourself a sweetheart in town?"

"No, cello teacher."

"Right. Elaine's cello."

"Who was Elaine again?"

"James's wife. She loved that cello. Back in their Buddhist days she used to say it was the only material possession she couldn't forsake."

"Do you think Elaine might want it back?" I asked, my voice tight. I didn't really want to hear the answer to my own question.

Cecelia looked at me. "James never talked to you about her?"

"We weren't that close. Just met over the car, like I said."

"Elaine was killed in a car accident, what, seven years ago now, this Christmas. So was Eliza, their daughter."

"Oh no, I'm so sorry. I didn't know."

"How could you know? James isn't known for talking about himself. Like I said, I barely even know where he is most of the time."

"You said before he had two kids, though?"

Cecelia nodded. "A son. He was in a car with James right behind Elaine and Eliza when a semi hit Elaine's little Volkswagen. Isaac was only three when it happened. I'm not sure how much he remembers."

"Isaac was there, too?"

"Isaac is James's son. My nephew. Didn't I mention that?"

"I must have missed it."

"I took Isaac right after the accident. James just couldn't … cope. He was supposed to come and get him when he got his shit back together, but I guess that hasn't quite happened yet. I've stopped holding my breath. Seth and Isaac are inseparable, like brothers. And Isaac needs me. I don't think being raised by a single father who's a hermit living in a rusty old bus is the ideal situation for him. He's a very special boy. James has never been able to relate to Isaac, even since before the accident. He's the spitting image of his mother."

"That's very nice of you, raising your brother's kid for him. He's lucky he has you. They both are."

"I wouldn't have it any other way. It's how it's supposed to be. Isaac has lots of people who love him. Maybe that's God's way of making it up to him, for taking his mother and sister. It's not like any of us planned for things to turn out like this, but sometimes life gets in the way of all your plans."

I couldn't tell you everything we got to talking about after that, and I can't place the exact moment when the talking turned into something else altogether. By that time we were in the living room, listening to Tom Waits records and finishing that bottle of wine. Cecelia cracked the front window open and we stood in a swirl of draft, swapping drags off one cigarette and trying to blow all the smoke outside. She kept saying she didn't want a whole one all to herself, she'd just have a puff off mine, if that was okay by me. Left a bit of vanilla lip balm on the filter. That was okay by me, too.

The next morning, I lay there in my motel bed for hours, shirtless and tangled up in the sheets, a permanent smile on my face, like a crack in the concrete. Rolled over on my side to scribble in my journal, the Beatles harmonizing through the tinny little speaker on the alarm clock radio. *Sunday, 9:35 a.m. The morning after. I can still smell her on my skin, and my tongue keeps finding the place inside my mouth where she bit my lip. Her silhouette haloed by the streetlight outside, how her sweater sent out little blue sparks into the dark when she pulled it over her head and shook out her braid. I've never been naked with a woman who had had a baby before. My fingers found and traced the shimmery lines left there in the skin of her belly, the ultra soft skin of her breasts. I never had sex like that with an almost stranger before. She had was so straightforward about it all. Put your hand here, Joseph. Here, I'll show you, like this.*

I decided my stitches could finally handle a shower. I leaned one arm against the cool tiles of the stall and let the almost scalding water needle down between my shoulder blades until my skin was glowing and humming.

We were laughing about something, I can't remember the details. She was one of those people who leaks tears from the corners of their eyes when they really crack up about something, and she kept wiping them away with the back of her thumbs. She was sitting next to me on the couch, to my right, and then without much ceremony and in mid-sentence she swung her right leg over her left one and across both of mine, planting herself in my lap, her face inches from mine. Her hands were warm and rough on my chest, under my shirt, pulling on the long end of my belt.

I flipped through the stack of snapshots I saved in my head of what happened after that, and what I remember next was my body going stiff all on its own, with no conscious help from me. She had me in her mouth, and she had reached with her other hand and slipped a spit-slicked finger into my ass. I froze, my hand tangled in the maze of her unbraided hair. She stopped, flashed her eyes at me. Left her finger right where it was.

"What's wrong, Joseph? Does that make you uncomfortable?"

"I'm not really sure. I don't know, exactly."

"Don't tell me you're forty years old and you haven't found your own prostate?"

"I've seen it on camera, at the doctor's. It's pinker than you might think."

Cecelia laughed. "Should I take it out?" She wiggled her finger, it called out come hither from its perch inside of me. "You don't like how that feels?"

"Did I say that?"

"So maybe you should shut up and relax."

I dried off, reminding myself to bring a towel from home when I came back here. Shaved in front of a steamy three-sided mirror, for the first time catching the deep purple hickey Cecelia Carson had deposited at some point in the hollow above my collarbone. I pressed it with my forefinger, watched it fill up with blood again. The muscles under my hips were stiff from remembering everything. I never would have made a move, as much as it had been in the back of my mind ever since the first time I saw her. I would have sat there tight all night with my hands folded in my lap, if it had been left up to me.

She hadn't asked me to stay, or even showed me her bedroom. We had laid there for awhile in a tangle on the rug in front of her couch, whispering and passing back and forth the red end of my last cigarette, just letting the smoke hang there in the dark above us. It was late, maybe one o'clock, and too cold now to open the window on our naked backs and legs.

Cecelia still had her fingers buried in my hair. "You should probably go. I have three nice ladies coming over at nine for our stitch and bitch. It's my week to be hostess."

I slipped out her front door and down the steps, my new shirt untucked and half-buttoned. I stopped at the 7-Eleven on my way back to the Capri, bought some smokes. Threw in a little magnetic checker game for Raylene.

I sat for a bit on the bench outside, my mind pulling wheelies and my lips still burning with her on them. I was going to have to wrap my head around quitting smoking again soon. I was really getting to love it again.

A thin rectangle of yellow light appeared in Hector's doorway, and a wide-shouldered man with black black hair slid through it into the dark and clicked the door shut behind him. The motion light on the stucco wall above our stretch of sidewalk popped on as he passed under it, hard lines lighting up his face as he crossed the lot, his cowboy boots sounding hollow in the still. He unlocked the door of a midnight blue Trans Am and I heard the dull damp thump of a subwoofer as his ignition kicked over. Guns N' Roses. Whoever this guy was, the solenoid on his starter was definitely about to pack it in.

By the time I finished my smoke and fished out my door

key on its plastic diamond, Hector had switched off the light in his room.

Fuck me, I thought. How come nobody ever tells me anything?

1:09 p.m. Later in the day of the morning after. I took a really long shower and then went straight over to Hector's, dragged him away from his cowboy novel and we walked across the highway to the truck stop all-day breakfast place beside the PetroCan. Found us a little upholstered hollow of a booth in the back. Two specials. Only one coffee. I wanted Hector to know that I was cool with it, with him. I wanted him to know I wasn't a redneck about stuff like that. That I didn't care. For some reason I needed him to know how much our little chats meant to me. How much he reminded me of my father sometimes.

Hector kept spinning a jam packet on its tin foil top on the table between us. One side of his suede collar was turned in, hugging the thin skin of his neck. The remnants of our breakfasts were stacked together and pushed to one side.

"I saw the first guy leaving your room a couple of nights ago. I was outside smoking, just so you don't think I've been snooping around in your business. I'm not like that."

The jam packet stopped under the square nail of his forefinger. He didn't say anything.

"And the guy last night, too. So I just want you to know that I'm not the kind of guy who makes a judgment about that kind of thing. I know we just met a couple of days ago, but I've already come to really value our friendship."

"Likewise, Joseph."

"So I want you to feel like you can be honest with me. I don't care about that stuff."

"What stuff would you be referring to?" Hector motioned for the waitress, stalling my answer as she whisked away our plates and refilled his cup.

"I don't care if you're gay."

"I don't use that word. I was married to a woman whom I adored for many years."

"Well, bisexual, then. You'll have to excuse me, Hector, I'm just a mechanic. Whatever you want to call yourself, that's okay by me too."

"I've never called myself much of anything. I've never felt the need to."

"Well, I just wanted you to know I was okay with it, whatever you want to call it or not."

"I appreciate the sentiment, Joseph. I want you to know that, I really do. I also must be honest, though, and tell you that it is really of no consequence to me if you are okay with how I choose to spend my private time or not. I taught myself not to care what other people think of how I live, many years ago now. I had to. We all have to, eventually. But thank you, all the same. Shall I ask for the bill?"

Hector insisted on paying for breakfast, acting insulted when I tried to stuff a rumpled ten-dollar bill into his coat pocket. He left the waitress a huge tip, and wouldn't meet my eyes.

Outside, the wind whipped across the chipseal, and a tiny tornado spun dust and garbage past the gas pumps and whirled itself through the parking lot, dying with a ripple in the tall grass that grew in the ditch beside the highway. The air smelled heavy and kind of metallic, like it might snow.

Hector flipped the collar of his coat up and lit a smoke, leaning into me, using my body to block the wind. We sprinted across the highway in between two big rigs, squinting our eyes against the wake of exhaust and cold air that swirled behind them as they passed by.

We walked back to the motel without another word, the square set of Hector's shoulders telling me to just keep my mouth shut. I guess I had stumbled across some unmarked line, and he was letting me know with every tight step he took that this conversation was definitely and permanently over.

He bid me a good day with a tip of an invisible hat and a curt nod, twisting the toe of his boot to put out his half-smoked cigarette, still not looking right at me. Pulled his door shut behind him with a click.

I stood there for a minute, staring at the brass numbers screwed to his door. Someone had replaced one of the brass screws with a cheap metal one at some point, and a trickle of rust bled from it, down the belly of the number eight and into the peeling blue paint.

I thought about knocking, stumbling through some kind of apology, telling Hector I meant well, that in the future I would mind my own business. Then I heard the chain lock slide into place on the other side of his door, and saw his curtains drawn all the way closed.

I let out a long sigh and unlocked my own door. The bed had been made, and my room smelled like Pine-Sol. I pulled off the white ring of sterilized paper from the toilet seat, balled it up and dropped it into the empty trash can. Thought about calling Cecelia. Ran my hands over the white, white towels that Lenny's wife had folded into perfectly uniform shapes and stacked on the wire rack next to the tub. I realized I didn't even know her name. Her towels were thin, smelled faintly of bleach. Nothing soft about them. I knew she was from somewheres in eastern

Europe by the sound of her accent; I wondered what she had dreamed about this new life in Canada, what she had packed to bring with her, what she had to leave behind. What she wrote about this place in her letters to her sisters, how often she was able to call home. What it would be like to watch your nieces and nephews grow up only in photographs. I tried to imagine Lenny being kind to her, maybe on a quiet night in the off-season, when the tourists were long gone south and a heavy snowfall had silenced the traffic on the highway. Tried to imagine him finally closing the always open door that was always open at the back of the motel office, the door that led from the cluttered front counter into their private lives. I tried to conjure up a picture of him, running her a bath, then sitting on the toilet seat next to her as they talked until tears of steam ran down the frosted glass of their bathroom window, talking until her fingertips were all wrinkled and soft. Him passing her a crunchy towel that smelled like bleach to wrap her wet hair in, and another to fold around the thin lines and long bones of her body. Her tucking a worn corner of white terrycloth under one armpit, the skin there soft and wobbly, showing the blue lines of her long life, just below the surface.

I went out to get some water from the pop machine next to the laundry room. Lenny was in the office, leaning back in his chair with his fingers laced together behind his head, both feet up on his desk. He dragged his gaze from the flickering television in the corner when he heard me come in, the bells on the door tinkling as it swung shut behind me. I slid a five across the counter, asked him for some change. Then I asked him what his wife's name was.

He narrowed his eyes, cocked his head to one side.

"What did she do now, she forget something? You need

anything, you just call me and ask, right? Like I told you before."

"My room is fine. She does a great job, I just wondered what her name was, so when I see her around, I could say hello, you know, properly."

"Her name is Petrovich, like my name. You call her that. Mrs Petrovich. But she don't talk much to the customers, my wife, she is afraid of her English. You need something, it's better you talk to me. Eleven years since we come to Canada, still she learns nothing in English." Lenny shook his head, like I should feel sorry for him. Like I understood his troubles.

I took my stack of coins and left. Mrs Petrovich's cart was parked in the courtyard next to the laundry room doors, and I followed the sound of a vacuum cleaner to a room whose door had been propped open with an old brick. She was inside, and looked a little startled when I waved at her from the doorway. She turned off the vacuum and stood up straight, tucked a stray bit of hair back behind her ear, nervous.

"You need more towels?" she almost whispered it, her eyes fixed on the carpet right in front of her feet.

I smiled wide. "I don't need a thing. I just wanted to thank you for your hard work. My room is always so clean, Mrs Petrovich. You do such a good job around here."

She covered her smile with one hand, and shooed me off with the other, shaking her head and blushing, suddenly ten years younger. Turned the vacuum back on to change the subject, waiting for me to leave before going back to work.

Back in my room, I opened my journal and thought for a long minute before picking up my pen.

4:10 p.m. Stress level: medium. Maybe a little bit high for a guy on holiday. Should have kept my mouth shut about the gay thing. What made me think Hector would care if I approved of his lifestyle anyways? Weather: cloudy, with a slow-moving cold front developing over breakfast. Mood: mostly mellow, with a bit of a breeze in my belly in the late afternoon, as my cello lesson gets closer.

The front of Caroline's house had a sideways grin on its di-lapidated face. The front stairs had once been given a thick coat of lipstick red, but now they sagged in a sorry pout, the paint long worn into the cracks. There was a loop of baling wire twisted into an oval noose that I had to lift off a picket in the fence to open the gate, leaving rust rings on my fingers.

I stood on the porch, the bottom of the cello case rest-ing on the top of my boot in the soft spot behind my steel toe, my journal tucked into the warmth under my arm. Two freshly sharpened pencils and a brand new eraser in my coat pocket. I was sucking on some Tic Tacs just in case, as I wasn't sure what kind of physical proximity might be involved in demonstrating proper cello technique.

I knocked on the door in three separate bursts, but there was no answer. Then I heard the gate squeak open and shut behind me.

"You must be Joseph? Sorry I'm late."

I assumed this must be Caroline, negotiating the baling wire loop around a backpack and a bunch of dry cleaning. Her dry cleaning bag got caught on the gate and she let forth a stream of swear words which would have made my mother blush, especially coming from a woman no older than twenty-five.

"This place should be condemned. Good thing it's so cheap."

She jangled up the walk towards me, wearing what I would estimate at a pound of bangles on each wrist, stacked like slinkies halfway up both arms. Her fingers all rings and black nail polish. She breezed past me, a huge ring of keys adding to the clatter, and unlocked the door, kicking it open with a knee-high boot. Went straight for the thermostat in the hallway, cranked it up.

"Fucking see my breath in here. Can't play the cello with gloves on. Come on in already, and close the door. Jeezus. I'll make us some tea while it warms up in here a bit. Don't worry about your boots."

She disappeared down a narrow hall wallpapered with band posters, blowing into her hands. She left her coat on, which looked like it was made from the same stuff they make those matching bathroom sets, except hers was dark violet, whereas the set in my mom's guest bathroom was more light pink, to match the little shell-shaped hand soaps you weren't actually supposed to wash your hands with, because they were matching.

I followed her into the kitchen, feeling weird for still wearing my boots all the way inside someone else's house. She came to a brief stop, just long enough for me to get a close look at her. Her face all angles, but somehow prettier than that sounds, a thumbtack of a nose, her lips wine-coloured, with an even darker outline, like a cartoon pin-up girl's mouth. Eyebrows thinned almost into obscurity. Black caterpillars for eyelashes, and what looked like super fine sparkles winking from her cheeks and chest. She rinsed out two mugs in the sink and lit a burner on the gas stove with a wooden match, blowing it out with a musical shake of her wrist.

"You don't look like how you sounded on the phone," she said.

"How's that?"

"You don't look like your average cello player, is all."

"I could say the same thing about you. Let me guess. I look more like the electric guitar type to you? That's what everybody else says."

"I was going to say banjo or fiddle, maybe, no offense."

"None taken. I'm Irish, or at least my grandparents were."

"I'm half-New York Jewish intellectual, half-Californian draft dodger. I've got the therapy bills to prove it. Is that a pack of cigarettes I see in your pocket? Wanna step onto the back porch and have one before we get started? I haven't had one all day. Work was a fucking nightmare."

She led me through a sliding glass door and we sat down in a couple of wooden chairs. The back deck was covered by a sighing frame of two-by-fours that supported a leaf-laden section of corrugated plastic roofing. The wooden railing around the deck was adorned with a rusting collection of mismatched metal bits, chrome hubcaps, and painted table-saw blades screwed to its flaking pickets, what looked like a fireplace grate bolted to the handrails, and strung with little Christmas lights shaped like chili peppers and cowboy boots and Mexican sombrero hats. My mother would have called it an eyesore and complained about bohemian renters driving down the property values, but I kind of liked it.

"So, task at hand, then. How long have you been playing the cello?"

I counted on my fingers, tapping them on the knees of my corduroys. "Going on two whole weeks, now."

"What made you pick the cello? Most of my students are rich little twelve-year-old brats with mothers from the ladies' auxiliary."

"It's my mother's fault. She's been all over me lately to

191

get a hobby, and the cello just sort of came along at the right moment, I guess. Traded a car for it." I lit two cigarettes and passed her one. "But I actually really like it, and I want to learn how to play it the right way," I added, just in case she thought I wouldn't be a dedicated student. "Like, proper technique and what have you. Need some direction."

"That's what I'm here for. They don't call me the cello bitch for nothing."

"Is that what they call you?"

"Among other things. At work I'm the Ice Queen."

"Where do you work?"

"I'm a check-out girl at Red Hot Video. I only meant to work there for a couple of months, but here I still am, two years later. The customers love me because I abuse them. Porn addicts, they love the verbal abuse. My boss is so scared I'm going to quit that he lets me take whatever nights off I need to do gigs, no hassle, so I can't seem to leave. One of my roommates works there too. Beats making lattes."

"You must meet all sorts."

"Different versions of the same sort, more like. Business suit or steel-toed boots, they all have the same eyes. You get so you can see them coming a mile away. Our band wrote a song about it. The lyrics are all cheesy titles of movies. 'Back Door Betty,' it's called. You should check it out, I'll dig a CD out for you before you go. I'm playing electric cello on a couple tracks too. Is that the kettle? We should head in. My nipples are about to leave me behind."

This last part made me blush, which I tried to hide, so she wouldn't think I was uptight.

"It's starting to thaw in here a little. Should be warm enough to pull your cello out now. Bring your baby in, let's take a look at it."

I retrieved the case from the hallway and laid it down in one corner of the kitchen. Caroline was pouring boiling water out of a saucepan into a chipped brown teapot. Covered it with a fabric cozy sewn in the shape of a fat tomato and sat it on the counter. She removed all of her bracelets and rings and laid them on the counter.

I brandished the cello in the fading daylight coming through the kitchen window. Its varnish glowed warm and red-brown. I had rubbed every last thumbprint in its finish off with the soft chamois before I had come over.

Caroline was pouring our tea into mugs. When she looked up, she sucked in her breath and reached out to take the cello from me. She let out a long, thin whistle.

"What kind of car did you say you traded for this?" She tilted it towards the light and peered through what I had recently learned were the F-holes.

"Late-eighties Volvo station wagon."

"Well someone got ripped off, and it wasn't you. Ebony fingerboard. Ivory fine tuners. I think the back and sides are mahogany. Usually it's maple."

"It's actually rosewood, I'm pretty sure."

"Rosewood? Never heard of that. It's a fucking beauty, Joseph. I've never seen one like it, ever. Mind if I tune it up and play it a little? Just to see what we're working with here?"

"I'd love to hear someone who knows how to play it. I mostly sound like a tomcat, so far."

"Hold this." She passed me the neck of the cello to hold while she ran upstairs with a thump of her boots, reappearing momentarily with a bow, which she tightened up as she walked.

She sat down on a straight-backed chair and spun the

cello seamlessly into position in the semi-circle between her thighs. Elbows akimbo, she lowered her head to bring the strings close to her ear, and thumped her thumb on the first string, cocking her head to one side. Then the next string, then all four. "When was the last time you tuned this thing? It's still perfectly in tune. That's weird, for November. Cellos don't usually like changes in the temperature much."

"I tuned it this morning, with my new fork. It's an 'A'."

"Well, you did a good job." She picked up her bow from the kitchen table, drew it towards her belly, her face a serious mask.

The cello sounded up with a sigh, and Caroline's left hand stretched like a spider on the fingerboard. I had never heard someone play the cello live in front of me, and I could feel the hair on my arms rise up inside my shirtsleeves as the sound thrummed alive in the floorboards beneath my feet. She played a few long low strokes, and then began shaping a melody with her fingers, her right hand a combination of strokes and taps with the bow, effortless and beautiful, mesmerizing, even. I found myself holding my breath, my lips parted and suddenly dry.

Caroline played for quite a while, and I watched her the whole time, her eyes closed, her shoulders moving gently in time with the music. She finished the classical-sounding tune she started off with, and then bent it into what I eventually recognized as a distant cousin of "Smoke on the Water." I hadn't heard that song since the summer after high school, doing bong hits in Dave Norris's mom's basement suite and playing air hockey. I liked it even better on the cello.

Then the fridge kicked in with a painful electric buzz,

and Caroline stopped short, her brows knit into a well-plucked zipper.

"That fucking goddamned bitch-ass of a kitchen appliance." She passed the back of her bow hand across her face. "I wouldn't mind so much if it whined in tune, but it's just a bit sharp to be a B-flat. It'll stop in a minute."

I ripped a bit of cardboard from a six-pack of empty Coronas stacked by the back door and used it as a shim to prop up one leg of the fridge a bit, which made the hum disappear.

"Well, aren't you handy. Why the fuck didn't I think of that? I've been bitching about that fridge for four years."

I shrugged.

Caroline sat back, spun the cello around, and ran her hands over its rounded back. "This is the most beautiful instrument I think I've ever touched. Like playing a stick of butter with a hot knife. What a beauty. You should have it appraised. It's probably worth a small fortune. Do you know where it came from? It looks older than mine, and mine originally belonged to my grandfather. He played first chair in the Toronto Symphony for years. He's the one who taught me, at first. He would've loved to have seen this. Look at the scroll work on the brass, and the inlay in the back. They definitely don't make them like this anymore." She leaned over and pressed her nose against it. "Smells like heaven. Have you smelled it?"

I nodded. I actually had. A mix of beeswax and hardwood and something sweet, like honey or chocolate, which hung in your nostrils for a bit, like warm angel food cake. I felt oddly puffed up with pride, like I had built the thing myself.

"All I know is that it belonged to the wife of the guy I got it from. She died in a car accident a while ago."

"I'd offer to buy it from you but there's no way I can afford it. Just don't ever let it collect dust in a closet, or I'll be forced to bitchslap you. An instrument this beautiful deserves to be played and taken care of. You have to love it like your wife."

"I'm divorced."

"Just as well. She'd only be jealous. This cello is a fucking masterpiece, Joseph. I hope you have house insurance. Don't ever leave it in your car. I could tell you a million tragic tales."

I nodded, solemn. She was the preacher, and I was the requisite sinner.

Caroline shook her head, pushed the neck of the cello in my direction. "Sorry, Joseph, I got carried away. You're not paying me good money to sit there and watch me slobber all over your instrument. Let me go grab mine, here, pull up a chair beside me, and we'll start with proper body position. We should get down to it, my roommates will be home by four-thirty, and all chaos will break loose."

I slipped another couple of Tic Tacs in my mouth and sat with my cello between my legs, trying to mimic the relaxed stance that Caroline had just demonstrated. I felt thick-fingered and clumsy, all wrong angles and thumbs. Caroline sat back down next to me, and peered over her strings at the position of my legs and arms.

"Now, straighten up your back, and plant both feet on the floor, solid, like. Good. Now position the neck so it rests against your right thumb, about an inch above your shoulder. Like that, yeah, good. Put the bow down for a minute, though, we'll get to that bit in a minute here. First things first. Pluck your first string, in open position, with your first finger." She showed me the same on her cello. "Good, we're relatively in tune. Now press down on that same string with your first finger, try to make it sound like this."

I did exactly as she told me, so excited I forgot to even feel self-conscious.

"Good, good ear, Joseph. You're a natural, see? Now alternate between those two notes, on my count of four ... two, three, four." She tapped the worn hardwood floor with the round black toe of her boot, and I plucked along slow beside her. "Now try the same thing on the next string over."

We went on like that for quite a while, until I learned the first two notes on all four strings, and then she made me do it while I spoke the names of the notes out loud in time.

"C-D-C-D-G-A-G-A-D-C-D-C-A-B-A-B and again, from the top." Caroline stood up, her cello resting on its endpin, and walked around me, lifting my elbow with one finger and kneading my right shoulder so I relaxed and dropped it a bit. I plucked away, my tongue resting in the corner of my lips to help focus.

The next hour passed by like this, easy.

I could barely force myself to stop and look up when the front door burst open and a scruffy little dog skittered into the kitchen, its whole ass moving in a furious wag.

"Don't pet the fucking mutt. She piddles when she gets excited." This from the tall woman who appeared in the doorway to the kitchen, wearing camouflage pants and a black leather jacket. She stomped over to the table and slipped her hands under the tomato tea cozy, pressing them around the still warm ceramic.

"Joseph, this is Amelia, one of my roommates," Caroline said. "Is it four-thirty already?" Caroline stood up and stretched the small of her back, placed her cello back into its case, propped it up in the corner. "I guess we should pack it in for today." She washed out another mug from the sink, placed it in front of Amelia. "How was your shift?"

Amelia rolled her eyes. "Suspenders Man came in and tried to return a DVD with a big thumbprint of a comeshot, right smack in the middle of the disc. Jacko totally almost popped a blood vessel in his head when he saw it. Banned the guy for three days. Sorry, Joseph. Daily debriefing."

I nodded, unsure how to follow that.

"We'll get to the bow next time, Joseph," Caroline said. "You did great. You want to book the next lesson now?"

I stood up, carried my cello over to its case. "You busy next Sunday? I'm coming back to Calgary next weekend. I'd love to do this regular, like, before I forget everything I learned."

"Same time then? I'll photocopy some sheet music before then for you too, now that I know where you're at. You like Deep Purple?"

I nodded.

"Just practice what I taught you today as much as you can until then. Until you can do it without looking at your left hand."

"Can I borrow your washroom before I head out?"

"First door at the top of the stairs. The hall light is burnt out, so watch you don't step on the cat."

In the bathroom, there was a stack of *Utne Readers* and some incense matches on the tank lid. I pissed for what seemed like a long time, taking care not to backsplash and gently replacing the seat in the downright position. Lit an incense match, just to see what amber smelled like. Smelled kind of like the cello did.

I headed back downstairs and towards the kitchen, and heard the two of them talking.

"Kind of cute, in a truck-driver sort of way."

"Not to mention his million-dollar cello, and a good ear. Picks stuff up right away."

I rounded the corner into the kitchen, and they both stopped short.

"That was quick. I didn't even hear you coming." Caroline swallowed, and looked at Amelia.

I held up my wrists and shook them, naked except for my gold watch. "No bangles. Nice to meet you, Amelia."

I picked up my cello and tucked my journal under my arm. Caroline followed me to the front door.

"That was fun. I learned a lot," I said. I fumbled in my front pocket for my cash. "So two hours is sixty, right?"

"Right. And I'll see you next week. You take good care of that baby, you hear me?"

"Beg your pardon?"

"The cello. Treat it like you would a baby."

"The cello. Right." I let out my breath. "I will."

Then the door closed, and there was just the sound of her tall boots walking away.

The whole city of Calgary seemed wrapped up in a sordid affair with the strip mall. I found one with a liquor store in it on my way back to the Capri and pulled over to get a bottle of something for dinner. Then I thought about how maybe bringing Kelly a bottle of wine might remind her of how she had no wine goblets, just plastic glasses with *Spider-Man 2* graphics and McDonald's logos on the side. Plus I thought red might not go too well with pork chops and mushroom sauce, and white wine always made my lips go numb and my face break out in a weird speckled rash. I settled on a six-pack of beer, and four of those cranberry vodka coolers, so she'd have a selection.

The Capri's parking lot was close to empty since it was Sunday night and the weekend traffic had moved on. Hector's truck wasn't there, and almost all the other rooms looked empty, curtains drawn against the dark. I stopped in my room for a minute to brush my teeth and re-apply some deodorant, and I grabbed the little gift I had bought for Raylene on my way out the door.

Kelly came to the door wearing an apron that said THAT'S NO WAY TO TREAT A LADY in block letters, over a pair of jeans and a baby blue sweater. She had her hair pulled back into one of those weird hair things with the wire inside of them, the same colour as her sweater. Raylene was looking freshly scrubbed and content, colouring in her book on the bed closest to the door. I took my boots off, noticing a new pair of miniature red shoes with buckles lined up beside her pink rubber boots on the snow mat behind the door.

201

"You get yourself some new shoes, Raylene? They sure are pretty."

"Gramma brought me them. Plus some new felt pens. They smell like their colour, too."

She held up a fat blue marker in my direction. I leaned in to sniff. Sure enough, blueberry, sweet, like Kool-Aid.

"Neat."

Raylene bent her arm back towards her own nose, nodding and bouncing a little on the bed. I noticed a blue streak under one nostril, and a matching orange one on her upper lip. She was in her little feety pajamas already. I sometimes secretly wish they made flannel pyjamas with feet sewn right in them, men's size large.

This kid was starting to seriously grow on me. So not spoiled, unlike Sarah's kids. Every toy under the sun, and still always lamenting how bored they were.

I passed Raylene the 7-Eleven bag. "I got you something, too. Just a little game of checkers. I thought maybe I could teach you how to play."

I set the beer and coolers down on the TV table. Kelly's work uniform was laid out on the only chair, her gold name tag with the Esso logo pinned on it and a box of tampons placed squarely on top.

Kelly fussed around a bit then, helping Raylene pry open the plastic package and remove the checkerboard, and putting a couple beers in the mini-fridge. "Say thank you to Joseph for the present, Bug," Kelly said, then turned to me. "You don't need to be buying us anything, Joseph, I'm supposed to be paying you back with this supper." She played up being annoyed, but her face glowed a pleased colour of pink. "I need to go check on our dinner."

Turned out Mike's Hard Cranberry Lemonade was

Kelly's all-time favourite, how did I know, and Raylene already knew how to play checkers, but had left her old set on the Greyhound, plus this new one had Snakes and Ladders if you flipped it over, which was her favourite game in the whole world next to Hungry Hungry Hippos, which her cousins had but she was probably going to get for Christmas anyways, right, Momma?

Kelly had put down a tablecloth and laid the table with three differently patterned plates. There was an empty juice bottle with two flowers made from pipe cleaners in it for a centrepiece. During dinner, she took sips of her vodka cooler, leaving lipstick marks on the rim of her plastic glass. She seemed kind of nervous. Raylene asked me if I could cut up her pork chop for her in such a bell-like little voice it tapped on my breastbone. At one point, Kelly made Raylene laugh until milk came out of her nose, and Raylene bolted into the bathroom for a Kleenex, her plastic pyjama footies whistling on the indoor/outdoor carpeting.

Dinner was perfect, right out of the can, just like my mom used to make on nights when I had a hockey game. Pork chops in mushroom sauce, a little cluster of cauliflower and broccoli and baby carrots, the frozen kind from a plastic bag, which Raylene pushed around her plate with the back of her fork.

Later, I was halfway through letting the kid beat me at Snakes and Ladders when she conked out, flat on her stomach with both hands folded under her chin. Looked like she was pondering her next move, except she was snoring.

Kelly picked her up and spun her end for end, then tucked her into bed, tugging the covers up around her daughter's round little flushed face. Raylene stuck her felt-penned thumb into her mouth in her sleep. Kelly pulled it out, Raylene put it back. Kelly pulled it out again and tucked her little matchstick of an arm under the covers, right next to the stuffed moose.

We both watched her slip into sleep for a minute or so, her feet twitching under the covers. She shifted a bit, freeing one arm from the sheets. Her fingers found the satin trim on the motel blanket and she rubbed it between her thumb and first finger.

Kelly let out a long sigh. "She's been wired for sound all day. Tony's mom gave her cream soda. That stuff is like crack for a six-year-old. Wanna step out for a cigarette?"

Kelly unfolded two camping chairs outside on the sidewalk, shifting the leg of one around to avoid the cracks in the concrete. "And Grandma got us another smoking chair, too, in case of company."

"She went all out, huh?"

Kelly snorted and didn't respond, waiting for me to light the twist of paper at the end of her machine-rolled smoke.

"I think I ate too much," Kelly said, puffing out her cheeks. She tapped her ash into the palm of her hand, then tipped it onto the concrete between her slippers.

"Thanks a lot for the home-cooked meal, Kelly. I had a fun time with you and Raylene. I really dig her, she's a sweet kid. You're doing a great job, you know, all on your own and all."

"I wish someone would tell her evil grandmother that. She showed up here today without even calling, like fucking Mother Theresa with a bad perm, made us go to Wal-Mart with her to buy us a bunch of crap, like cereal and juice and stuff we haven't even run out of yet and making little hints that I can't afford to feed my own kid or whatever."

"Maybe that's just her way of trying to be supportive."

"She looked at my hair and said if I couldn't afford a haircut, I should just tell her and she'd pay for it. I spent the afternoon trying not to drill her in the head when she wasn't looking. On account of she's really the only family Raylene has. Her daddy could give two fucks about her. Haven't heard from him since he left, not once, plus he probably won't live to turn thirty, the rate he's going."

"The crystal meth," I said, nodding down at the concrete.

"Hector blabbed to you about that? I told you that guy knows too much about everything. He drags it out of people."

"He was only telling me how much he thought of you, all on your own with the two jobs and the kid and everything."

"Yeah, like I'm some kind of novelty item. Like I'm the only single mom in town. Look around, I always tell him, we're all over this neighbourhood. Only two of the kids in Raylene's daycare have daddies that live in the same house as them." Kelly took a long drag and squinted her eyes against the curl of smoke that blew back at her.

"Hector came around so much when we first got here I thought he was some kind of pervert, until I figured out he was gay, and just trying to be nice to everyone so he could write their life story into his book."

"You ever talk to him about the gay thing at all?"

"He doesn't call it gay. Hector says we all have a bit of gay in us, so it doesn't need its own word, or some such thing. Lenny, on the other hand, says a cocksucker is a cocksucker is all a faggot to him."

"What do you think?"

"I couldn't give a flying fuck, to tell you the truth. I had sex with a girl one time, this chick that Tony and I picked up at his cousin's wedding. I drank too much lemon gin and barely remember anything, but Tony said we had a great time, her and I and him. Whatever, no big deal. We had to drive her back to Edmonton in the morning because we slept in and she missed her ride back home. What the fuck do I know? She seemed cool about it all, real respectful, not acting like she owned him the next day or anything. That would have pissed me off. Hector ever try anything with you?"

"Nope. Never. Not even close."

"Didn't think he would. You don't look like the type, anyways. Your fingers are too big."

"How do you know that?"

"Not small, like, not short, but skinny. Skinny and long. Slender. Slim." Kelly made a stretching motion, starting from the fingertips of her other hand.

"Is that a scientific fact? Did they do a study on it?"

"Just a theory I have, something I've noticed. Check out Hector's next visitor. Long skinny fingers on him, I guaran-fuckingtee you. See for yourself."

"What about lesbians, what do their fingers look like?"

Kelly laughed out loud. "Well, with them you gotta consider the footwear. The warehouse at work is riddled with them. Workboots, or Dayton's, or hikers. Nine times out of ten. And belt buckles. The butchier ones, that is. The more girlie types, sometimes you can't even tell. I met some at our Christmas party, I would never have known without the workboot ones hanging around lighting their cigarettes and stuff."

"You seem to know quite a bit about gay people."

"I work in retail." Kelly reached over and pinched my

lighter from between my thumb and forefinger, lit another one of Hector's cigarettes.

We sat there and smoked in the quiet, that city kind of quiet, a little bit of traffic in the background, like a radio, and the rise and fall of sirens, so often you don't really hear them after a while. I was learning to like city quiet, since it did have its own version of still, its own nature sounds.

"Joseph?" She raised the end of my name in a question.

"Yeah?"

"There's something I want to tell you, I been thinking about it all day, in the back of my mind, but I don't want you to take it the wrong way."

"I'm listening."

"Well, first off I want to tell you that I think you're a totally super nice person, and Raylene, she just thinks you're the cat's ass, and we both like hanging out with you a lot, don't get me wrong."

Kelly paused, like she was nervous to say what was coming next.

"And I think you're pretty cute and all, and I don't even mind that you're … quite a bit older than me. But I've been thinking it all over, and I just thought I should tell you that I'm not looking to get involved with anyone right now, I just think that I need to keep focused on work and school, and I'm not available for any kind of relationship."

She flicked her ash again, and glanced at me sideways to see if I was still listening. I was.

"So I just thought I should let you know, you know, where I'm at with things, before you got your hopes up or anything, or spend your money on us for nothing. Raylene is going to be choked up about it. She wants us to get married, so she can carry the ring on a pillow. I don't know where she gets that from. Off the TV, I guess. Tony never gave me a ring. Mostly he just laid around in his underwear screaming at us to keep the noise down. It's no wonder she thinks you're Prince Charming. She's only ever seen you wearing pants. Kinda pathetic, if you think about it too much. Anyways, just thought I'd let you down easy, right at the beginning, like."

"I appreciate you being so honest with me, Kelly."

"I hope you won't let this affect our friendship."

"Course not. I'm really glad you cleared that up."

Kelly let out a long breath, put out her smoke, clapped her hands together to warm them up. "I should probably have a bath and get to bed. I'm opening tomorrow."

"I thought you had Mondays off?"

"Overtime. Plus once I've got five hundred hours I get part of my medical and dental covered by work. Raylene needs a retainer from sucking on her thumb. Night, Joseph."

At first it looked like she was going to move to hug me, and then she changed trajectory in mid-air and shook my hand, pressing it between both of her cold ones.

"You want the rest of your beers to take home with you? Or a cooler?"

I told her she should keep them in her little fridge, for the next time I came for a visit.

Hector's truck was back, tucked into its usual spot, its engine knocking and clicking into the dark as it cooled down. I could hear jazz music thrumming faintly from his side of the wall as I let myself into my room. The message light on the telephone flashed in the dark.

I took off my boots, stashed my cello in the closet, and called Lenny.

"Message for room 119, where did I put it? Oh yeah. Please call Cecelia if you get back before eleven tonight."

I thanked him and hung up. It was just after ten.

Cecelia picked up after four rings, just as I was rehearsing what I was going to say to her voice mail.

"Hello?"

Just that one word from her, and my stomach rolled over onto itself.

"Uh, hello, Joseph here. Joseph Cooper."

She laughed, and the knot in my tongue started to come untied.

"Hi there, Joseph. I was hoping it was you."

"I was hoping it was you, too. I mean, I was hoping you were home. I was going to call you earlier, but then I wasn't sure how soon was too soon, and so then I didn't, and then it got later, and I didn't know how late was too late, so anyways, it's good you called me. What I mean is, it's good. I'm glad you called." So much for being smooth, I thought.

"Joseph. Chill out. You're going to hyperventilate. It's just me."

"Chill. Right. Okay." She waited for me to say something that made more sense. I didn't.

"Joseph? You still there?"

"Me? Yeah. Right here. Sorry. I'm just, well I'm not so good on the phone. Never have been. Especially when I'm nervous. I'm better in person. I think. At least, I hope I am." My voice trailed off, and then another overripe silence hung between us for a bit.

Finally, Cecelia cleared her throat. "Then maybe you should just come over here."

"I was hoping you would say that. I mean, not that I assumed that you would...."

"Joseph. Shut up and put your boots on. I'll see you in a minute."

I was trying to think of something else to say, but then I heard a click, and the dial tone hummed into my ear.

I started up my truck exactly fourteen minutes later, my hair still wet. The stitches in my head were itching, and my T-shirt was stuck to my back because I hadn't dried off enough before jumping into my last clean change of clothes.

The roads sparkled with frozen dew. Hardly any traffic all the way over, just me and the odd taxi, our exhaust pipes trailing fat clouds of white smoke into the night.

I knocked softly on her door with one knuckle, and she opened it right away, wearing an old army sweater and faded jeans. Somehow even more beautiful than I remembered. She pulled me inside by one elbow, and I felt my skin stretch and tingle where she touched me. I followed her as she padded down the hall into the living room, her feet bare, trailing a faint trace of perfume behind her.

She motioned for me to sit down on the couch, and

grabbed an ashtray from the top of the stereo and placed it on the coffee table. She sank into the couch next to me with a sigh. I shifted my butt a little to close up the space between us. She leaned in and kissed me, her lips soft and a bit cold at first. Left a faint taste of cherry lip balm behind when she sat back and smiled at me.

I looked around the room feeling I had just woken up. Patted my pockets to find the familiar square of my cigarettes. Took one out, but didn't light it.

"Cecelia, I need to talk to you about something, before we … well, I have something I need to tell you."

She sighed, then reached out and pinched the cigarette from my fingers and put it in her mouth. I lit it for her, and she took a long drag and passed it back to me, waving one hand in front of her face to keep the smoke out of her eyes.

"Is this the part where you tell me you're not interested in a relationship, that you just want it to be casual? Or is this the part where you ask me if I'm seeing anybody else, or if I do this kind of thing all the time?"

"Actually, I wanted to talk to you about Jim."

"My brother?"

I nodded. I offered her another drag but she didn't want one, so I crushed the butt out in the ashtray.

"I told you when we first met that I was looking for your brother because he left his car with me. But that was only partly true. I didn't lie, I just didn't tell you everything."

Cecelia looked at me, said nothing.

"So maybe this is nobody's business but Jim's, and maybe I should just keep my mouth shut, I don't know, but I'm pretty sure the right thing to do is tell you the whole story. I didn't come here because your brother left a used car behind. I came here because he dumped something way bigger than that on me. I mean, I don't think he meant to, but that's what he did."

She still didn't say anything, so I kept going.

"So. I'm only going on circumstantial evidence here, but when I went out to Jim's place to have a look at the car right after it broke down, well, there was a chunk of hose and some duct tape in the trunk, and the whole inside was covered in soot. And, well, I'm no detective or anything, but it looked to me like he was trying to ... well, it looked to me like it was a damn good thing the car broke down when it did. So maybe a smarter guy would've just stayed out of it, but I couldn't. Couldn't not do anything. So here I am. I thought you should know. Maybe you could, you know, talk to him or something? I don't know what I thought I was going to do. I barely know the guy. But I couldn't let him just disappear, right? And then spend the rest of my life wondering what else I should have done."

Cecelia's eyes got shiny, but she blinked back the tears.

"You really are a good guy, aren't you? I guess I should have told you a few things last night, too. But I didn't realize ... I didn't think you needed to know. You said you didn't really know Jim, and I didn't realize it happened in the car."

"He told you?"

She nodded. "He spared me the details. Showed up here last week, dumped his stuff, and then checked himself into the psych ward. He'll be there for a while yet, and then he's going to take it from there. Maybe move into my basement for a while, just to have some family around. That seemed to work last time."

"He's done this before?"

"Last time it was pills. About a year after the accident. He never got over it, losing Elaine and Eliza. Not that anyone ever would. But it just crushed him. He was a paramedic. Did you know that?"

I shook my head, fished the half cigarette out of the ashtray and lit it, wishing I had a beer.

"The coroner said they were both killed instantly so it's not like there was anything James could have done to save them. One of the cops who was there told me that they found James just sitting on the guardrail, staring into space. Blood all over him. Isaac was still in his car seat, screaming blue murder. The cop said they couldn't get James to say a word, could barely get him to move. That was seven years ago, and he's still pretty much like he was that first night. Barely moving."

Cecelia stopped talking for a minute, and we shared the rest of my smoke in sad silence.

"You look very handsome tonight Joseph," she said at last, changing the subject. "Can I get you anything? A beer, maybe?"

"You read my mind."

She leaned forward and kissed me. This time, I kissed her right back.

Monday morning. Trying to think of things to write in my stress journal is kind of stressing me out. I'm thinking maybe I can tell the shrink I'm all cured up; that I got laid, I got a cello lesson, and I'm going to be a daddy. That it seems like everything is kind of sorting itself out. She'll probably tell me I'm in denial or repressing my real emotions or whatnot, but it's true, I feel like a whole new man. My dad used to say that after he had a shower or got a haircut or something. How he felt like a whole new man. Forgot how nice it was, to sleep in the same bed with someone else, someone who doesn't shed and bark in his sleep. I can still smell her perfume on my T-shirt.

Mood: whole new man.

I heard three short raps at my door. I opened it and Hector passed me a to-go cup of coffee, still so hot I had to pass it back and forth between my two hands so I didn't burn myself.

We sat on the bench outside for a couple of minutes, smoking and talking about the weather and when I was going to be back in Calgary, stuff like that. Neither of us mentioned our previous conversation, and that was just fine by me. I figured trying to talk about how I had already said too much might not be the best approach. I knew that him bringing me a coffee was his way of saying everything was still cool with us, and so I just drank it and let the sun feel good on my face.

Hector left to take care of some business, and I went back into my room and called Allyson. The voicemail picked up, which was what I was hoping for. I had rehearsed exactly what I was going to say.

"This is a message for Ally, and for Kathleen, too. It's Joey here, and I was just calling to see if either of you happened to know of a child's car seat that would fit into the front seat of a 1997 F450 Super Duty V8 Turbo Diesel Automatic tow truck, preferably one that would still leave room in the cab for a kind of large, smelly husky dog and a middle-aged male driver? Call me back and let me know. Looks like I'll be needing one in about six or seven months from now. Any information you have would be very helpful. Thank you."

I pressed the hang-up button on the phone, feeling kind of smart-assed and proud of myself. The phone rang while still in my hand, startling me. It was Dr Witherspoon's office saying that the doctor had been called out of town and asking if I could reschedule my three o'clock appointment. I said I would have to call back later in the week when I knew for sure when I would be back in town, trying to sound disappointed. I hung up.

I packed up my stuff, loaded my bag and the cello into the truck, and walked over to the office to check out. I told Lenny I'd be back next Friday, and he promised me he would try to keep 119 empty for me when I returned.

"Home sweet home, right?" He smiled from one side of his mouth as he passed me back my credit card. I felt sorry for Mrs Petrovich all over again.

The boxy blue and white shape of the Capri Motor Court shrank and then disappeared in my rearview mirror as I drove up the on-ramp and squeezed the truck into the traffic heading east. The city turned into rolling hills scabbed over with suburbs, and then the farmland took over, and the sky opened wide on both sides of the highway. I cranked up the Johnny Cash and rolled my window all the way down, stuck my left hand out and let it catch the wind, scooping and dipping the cold blue day between my fingers.

Every time I drove this road it reminded me of a thousand other trips home. There used to be a fruit stand next to the cut-off where my dad and I would stop and get cherries for my mom on our way back from doing business in Calgary. It was a gas station now, complete with a Tim Horton's and a car wash big enough to pull a motor home through.

Rick Davis and I had dragged our hungover asses back up this highway more than a few times, after weekend trips to the city to see a concert or to buy Christmas presents. I drove him home after his hernia operation a couple of years ago. He was stoned on codeine and lamenting about how old we were getting, how we used to only come to the city to do fun things, not like now, when he only got out of Drumheller to see the specialist or his lawyer. How he'd still take his wife back in a second, if she'd have him, even after everything that went down, but don't ever tell her that.

Allyson and I had driven a rental car home from the Calgary airport right after our honeymoon, tanned and laughing and kissing at all the stoplights. It was almost dark, in early summer. We had the windows down and the smell of clean hay and sage and manure and rain made us glad to be back in Canada. The streetlights lit up and faded around her profile as we drove, and I thought she was perfect. Thought we were perfect.

Drumheller appeared in front of me before I felt ready to be home. Small towns have a way of taking the very thing or person you were most hoping to avoid running into and stuffing it right up your ass at the earliest possible opportunity. I had just pulled off the highway and turned onto the main drag when he appeared in my windshield, standing right there in the middle of the crosswalk in front of the bank. Mitch Sawyer slapped the hood of my truck with one hand and motioned for me to pull over.

I took a deep breath and angle parked in front of the dollar store. He squeezed along the driver's side of my truck and rested one hand on my side mirror, chewing on a stir stick and squinting into the sun.

"Dude. I saw your mom at Safeway last night. Said you were in the city. Did you run into the muff-divers?" He stuck out his tongue and waggled it up and down.

I felt like drilling him right there in the middle of Main Street. Instead, I reached out and adjusted my mirror, forcing him to step back and take his hand off my truck.

"I saw Ally and Kathleen a couple of times. I'm going back next weekend. You want me to give them your regards?"

He laughed, like I was making a joke that we were both a part of. The guy still hadn't figured it out that I couldn't stand him. Thought we were partners in the same misery.

I told him I had to go meet Franco, and backed my truck up before he could say anything else. It was twenty after twelve. I knew exactly where to find Franco. He never got around to making a lunch on Sunday night. Sunday was the night he played poker at the Legion, so he'd be at Ida's, in the last booth by the window, halfway through his clubhouse sandwich and fries. Black coffee with one sugar. Water with no ice. I'd go find Franco, and he'd tell me how business was good, even better than when I was around, just getting in his way. Tell me how he didn't miss me a bit. Then we would go back to the shop and I would have to rescue all my new wrenches out of Franco's toolbox so I could get some work done.

I watched Mitch take the corner by the drugstore, hiking his jeans up over the wedge of white hairy ass that threatened to escape from under his jean jacket whenever he took a step.

Maybe I wasn't sure exactly what I wanted to be when I grew up, but at least I had figured out what I wasn't going to be.

Acknowledgments

First of all, I need to thank my partner Mette Bach, for the dinners and the back pats and the dog walks and the domestic bliss that made finishing this book possible. I have only ever written short stories before this, and I literally could not have done this without her belief in me. My deepest love and gratitude goes out to my cousin Dan Bushnell, for being the other fearless artist in a family that wishes both of us had pension plans. Not only does he keep me on track during the lean times, he is also the one who pried the hard drive out of my melted computer after my house burned down and saved this manuscript from joining the long list of things I lost that day. I also want to thank again all of the friends, colleagues, and especially strangers who helped me recover from the aforementioned house fire; without their love and support this project might never have survived, or been seriously delayed. I also want to thank Brian Lam, Robert Ballantyne, Shyla Seller, Nicole Marteinsson, Tessa Vanderkop, and Janice Beley and the rest of the folks at Arsenal Pulp Press for all their hard work and continued support over the last eight years. Lorraine Grieves and Cris Derkson for the cello tips. Sheri-D Wilson and my sister Carrie Cumming for the answers to my Calgary questions. Jan Derbyshire for the great late night novel read-off, and finally, the British Columbia Arts Council for keeping food on the table so I could write. I owe you all a million thank yous, and a steak dinner.

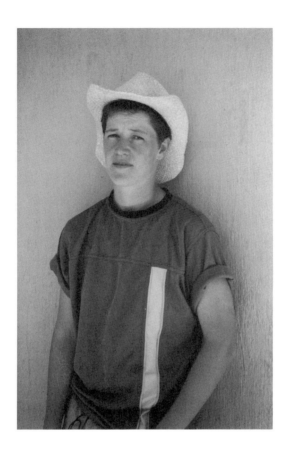

Ivan E. Coyote was born and raised in Whitehorse, Yukon and now lives in Vancouver. She is the author of three collections of short stories, all published by Arsenal Pulp Press: *Close to Spider Man*, *One Man's Trash*, and *Loose End*, which was shortlisted for the Ferro-Grumley Fiction Award in 2006. Ivan is also a renowned live storyteller. *Bow Grip* is her first novel.